CHICAGO PUBLIC LIBRARY
SULZER REGIONAL
4455 N. LINCOLN
CHICAGO, IL 60625

OCT   2006

Almost Eden

DISCARD

ANITA HORROCKS

Tundra Books

Text copyright © 2006 by Anita Horrocks

Published in Canada by Tundra Books,
75 Sherbourne Street, Toronto, Ontario M5A 2P9

Published in the United States by Tundra Books of Northern New York,
P.O. Box 1030, Plattsburgh, New York 12901

Library of Congress Control Number: 2005927006

All rights reserved. The use of any part of this publication reproduced,
transmitted in any form or by any means, electronic, mechanical,
photocopying, recording, or otherwise, or stored in a retrieval system,
without the prior written consent of the publisher – or, in case of
photocopying or other reprographic copying, a licence from the Canadian
Copyright Licensing Agency – is an infringement of the copyright law.

Library and Archives Canada Cataloguing in Publication

Horrocks, Anita, 1958-
Almost Eden / Anita Horrocks.

ISBN-13: 978-0-88776-742-5
ISBN-10: 0-88776-742-7

1. Mennonites--Juvenile fiction. I. Title.

PS8565.O686A64 2006   jC813'.6   C2005-902896-3

We acknowledge the financial support of the Government of Canada
through the Book Publishing Industry Development Program (BPIDP)
and that of the Government of Ontario through the Ontario Media
Development Corporation's Ontario Book Initiative. We further
acknowledge the support of the Canada Council for the Arts and the
Ontario Arts Council for our publishing program.

ONTARIO ARTS COUNCIL
CONSEIL DES ARTS DE L'ONTARIO

The author gratefully acknowledges the generous support of the Alberta
Foundation for the Arts and the Canada Council for the Arts.

Typeset in Janson

Printed and bound in Canada

This book is printed on acid-free paper that is 100% recycled,
ancient-forest friendly (100% post-consumer recycled).

1 2 3 4 5 6   11 10 09 08 07 06

R0408216285

CHICAGO PUBLIC LIBRARY
SULZER REGIONAL
4455 N. LINCOLN
CHICAGO, IL 60625

To Mom

CHICAGO PUBLIC LIBRARY
SULZER REGIONAL
4455 N. LINCOLN

1

How shines it?

I woke up knowing already that she was gone.

The baby robins outside my window were raising a real stink, trying to out chirp each other. "Feed me . . ." "Feed me first . . ." "No, me."

They had a nest tucked in the curve of the downspout, high under the eaves of our creaky old house. Not exactly the safest place Mom and Dad Robin could've picked to raise a family. You'd think they'd have figured that out after a thunderstorm blew their first batch out of the nest.

Mom was the one who found Tommy on the back porch guarding a mushy lump of feathers. She cried a little. Dad says Mom would cry over a mosquito. He says it like it's a bad thing. When she was done crying I helped her pick up three other dead baby birds from the sidewalk. She didn't want my little sister, Lena, to see them.

Grown-ups think they can hide things from kids. They think they can decide how much of the truth we're old enough to take. Like we won't figure it out on our own. Believe me, most of the time we know, even if we wish we didn't.

When my parents don't want me and my sisters to know what they're saying, they talk Plautdietsch, which is Low German. They were talking Plautdietsch last night, late. Loud enough for me and Lena to hear all the way upstairs in our room, even with the door closed and the blankets pulled over our heads.

I didn't want to think about that now. It was early still, too early for anyone else to be up. For a few seconds I lay in bed, my heart pounding a mile a minute, wondering what I should do. Then I couldn't take it anymore and scrambled out from under the covers to pull on some clothes. In the bed next to mine Lena whimpered. Her baby doll cheeks were rosy with sleep.

I didn't really give a care if I woke anyone up or not. Anyways, there was no point trying to avoid all the creaks and groans in our stiff old house. I slipped, barefoot, down the worn staircase, through the living room and kitchen into the back porch, flipped the hook on the door, and was out.

Tommy waited on the porch steps. Meowing, he curled around my bare leg like a furry grey muff. I stopped long enough to scratch behind his torn ear.

"*Voh scheent et?*" I whispered Dad's favorite greeting. "How shines it, Tom-cat? Someone will feed you soon." Except Mom was the one who always put out a bowl of milk in the morning. Dad refused to feed an alley cat.

Tommy shook off my hand and jumped up on the scaffolding next to the porch. Dad was painting the house and garage this summer. He'd gone out and rented the scaffolding and bought brushes and caulking and sandpaper and whatnot.

The scaffolding hugged the back of the house, looking a bit like it might sprout leaves. If I squinted a little I could almost see the vines twisting and curling until the house was totally hidden, like the castle in *Sleeping Beauty*. Which made me laugh, thinking that, because for sure there weren't any castles or Prince Charmings in Hopefield, capital of nowhere.

Swinging one leg over my bike, I coasted into the alley, making sure to check if Grandma Redekop was looking out her window. Grandma's room in the old folks' home across the alley looked right into our backyard. Us kids couldn't steal a pea pod out of the garden without Grandma knowing. She'd have a conniption fit if she saw me riding with no hands.

But it was too early for Grandma yet. The sun wasn't quite up, the sky still smeared with color. Cool morning air tickled my skin. Pedaling steadily, I let go. Loose gravel crunched under my bike tires.

At the end of the alley I made a wide sweeping turn onto the street and headed west, guiding the bike with my knees, back straight, arms dangling. Perfectly balanced, perfectly in control.

The first block, past the library, was easy. I'd been playing this game so long, one block didn't even count. So what if twelve was getting a bit old to play wishing games; I didn't give a care.

Riding two blocks with no hands was good for a small wish – something like pancakes for breakfast, the thin ones that you roll up with a fork. My friend Jillian called them crepes, but in our house they didn't have a fancy name. I wished for pancakes on Sundays, when Mom almost always made roll-up pancakes or waffles before church. On Saturdays – baking day – I wished for fresh cinnamon buns or maybe *kringel*, the soft white buns tied in curly knots, still hot out of the oven so that when my sisters and I bit into them the melted butter ran down our chins.

If I wanted my wishes to come true, I had to make them reasonable, not? I had to wish for things that "conditions favor." I'd learned that from reading *The Little Prince*.

Two blocks took me past the Mennonite Brethren church, which was right by where my school was, too. There was only one elementary school in Hopefield, and one high school. But there were six other Mennonite churches and one Lutheran church, too. We went to the MB. So did most of my friends, or else the Bergthaler

Mennonite or Grace Mennonite. A few were Sommer-felders. Jillian was the only one I knew who went to the Lutheran church.

I wished to make it another block, and another. Conditions favored my wish.

Three blocks with no hands meant I could make a bigger wish. Once I wished for an A on a social studies test – and got it. So what if I usually did; I was worried about that test, and my wish came true. So did the one where I wished that my sister Beth would break out in zits. Served her right. Just because she was four years older didn't give her the right to boss me around all the time.

Beth broke out in zits just before the Young People's campfire night where she was going with this guy she really liked. I'd felt a little bad about that one. I even asked God to forgive me. I didn't say sorry to Beth, though, so probably I still owed God one.

If I made it all the way from our house to the swimming pool, I could wish for anything my heart desired. It could be as unreasonable and far out as I wanted.

To get there I had to ride four blocks, go around two corners, over the railway tracks, down another two blocks, through a dip at the park entrance, and along the dirt road to the far end of the park. So far I'd never gotten farther than the railway tracks. This morning I wasn't even headed in that direction. I'd already passed the school and was almost up to Hippies Hangout, where my friends and I went almost every day after school to buy penny candy.

HONNNK!

Holy Moses. Talk about a heart attack. I grabbed the handlebars and slammed on the brakes, skidding to a stop. The driver glared at me, then backed the rest of the way out of his driveway and drove off. Like it was my fault that he didn't see me there in the middle of the road. *Fuy.*

Riding a bike with no hands was mostly pretty easy. Avoiding all the things that got in the way was the hard part.

I kept going, only now I was shaking too much to let go of the handlebars. Anyways, there were only fifteen blocks from one end of Hopefield to the other, so I was almost as far as I could go already. At the last intersection at the very end of town, I stopped. On this side of Valley Avenue, on one corner, was the old folks' home, the one that was the last stop before the cemetery a half-mile down the road. After that were fields of grain, rapeseed, and alfalfa. Lots of potatoes and beets and onions and corn, too. Hopefield was in the middle of one big garden that rolled north right up to Winnipeg and south to the U.S. border.

On the other corner on this side of Valley Avenue was a service station, still locked up tight so early in the morning. But across from the service station at the very edge of town, crouched an ugly squat building. Hunkered up against the floodway like a cornered cat, trying to hide. I liked that word. Hunkered. It fit perfect.

Lights flicked on here and there. Somewhere in that building was my mother. A shiver ran through me. Never mind how hard I tried not to think about it; I knew for sure that this time, she was there because of me.

I wondered if they made her wear a straitjacket.

Probably not, I told myself. Mom wasn't really crazy that way.

2

There are people, turtles, and three-cornered files

On the way home I rode down my friend Jillian's street, but it was way too early yet to knock on the door. Besides which, Jillian had slept over at Sadie's last night.

I should've seen it coming. Even if Mom *had* promised. Weeks ago already, when I'd first asked if I could have a pajama party on the last day of school. I'd waited until she was in a good mood, peeling vegetables for supper and singing along with the Johnny Appleseed record she'd put on the hi-fi for Lena. Mom got all excited when I asked.

"What a good idea!" She clapped her hands together. "We'll clean out the front porch for you and your friends. What do you want me to cook for everyone? Borscht maybe?" she teased.

"*Fuy*," I grimaced, which made Mom laugh. I knew a few words of my own in Plautdietsch. "Can we make pizza? With homemade sausage?"

"You can make anything you want, even Italian pizza with Mennonite sausage. We'll make you the best pajama party ever!" She laughed again, swinging me around the kitchen and singing, "*Oh, the Lord is good to me, and so I thank the Lord, for giving me the things I need, the sun and rain and an appleseed. Yes, He's been good to me.*"

We sang and twirled and sang until we were both laughing so hard my stomach hurt. Every time I thought I'd be able to stop laughing finally, Mom would break into another song like "She's Too Fat for Me," or "*Auch du Lieber Augustine.*"

Dad shook his head when he came home and we were still singing. "Calm down once, Esther," he said to Mom.

"Oh, you calm down," she laughed, going back to her vegetables.

That should have been my first clue. Mom was in too good a mood.

I'd invited everyone – Naomi, Heather, Joy, and Eleanor. And my best friends Sadie Heppner and Jillian Robb. I'd been best friends with Jillian all the way since her family moved to Hopefield three years ago, almost at the end of grade 3. It was 1967, because her first day in school was the same day as the pioneer pageant to celebrate Canada's 100th birthday. Everyone in the whole school was supposed to get dressed up like pioneers to honor our forefathers.

Jillian showed up in a cowgirl outfit, with a holster and gun and everything.

Our teacher, Mrs. Bergen, took her gun away. She said there was no such thing as a cowgirl, at least not around here. Besides which, guns had no place in a pacifist community, and she would be speaking to Jillian's parents.

That was during my Annie Oakley phase, so I was pretty sure Mrs. Bergen was wrong about there not being such a thing as a cowgirl. Only I never dared say so. Not to Mrs. Bergen. I told Jillian, though. I told her I wished I'd thought of being a cowgirl instead of wearing a stupid itchy bonnet and ugly long dress.

We'd been best friends ever since. It made me feel special to have a best friend who came from somewhere else. I was born in Hopefield, and so were all my other friends. And their parents, and even most of their grandparents, too. Or else close by in one of the dozens of little villages around here.

Anyways, for weeks already Jillian and Sadie and I had planned what we would do at my pajama party – swimming first, then pizza and records.

Last weekend I'd cleaned out the front porch all by myself because Mom had one of her sick headaches. I even scrubbed the bathroom and kept Lena out of the house and everything so Mom could have a sleep. And Beth had done the shopping and bought chips and pop and pizza mix and sausage for us. Everything was ready.

I tried not to worry too much yet. I just had to make sure to help out around the house and not fight with

Beth or Lena or anything, and then Mom would be okay again, not?

And I knew for sure she'd be happy when I brought my report card home. I thought I might even get a B in German, my worst subject ever. *Der, die, das* – what kind of language has three different ways of saying "the?"

In grade 4 once, I'd brought home a big fat F on my report card. Mom had been pretty good about it. "Never mind, Elsie," she said. "It's only one bad grade. You'll do better next time. Lookit, you got As and Bs in almost every other subject."

"I hate German! Why do we have to take it?"

"German is part of your heritage, part of who you are." Mom was rolling out dough to make ammonia cookies for Christmas. "Aren't you interested even a little bit in the language your ancestors spoke when they came here?"

I already knew the story. I already knew how my great-great-grandfather's family and a bunch of other Mennonites came here to Manitoba from Russia way back in 1874, because the government needed farmers so bad they were giving away land for next to nothing. And how the government promised them they could practice their religion and teach German to their children in school and everything. I'd known all of that and more, for as long as I could remember.

"That was a hundred years ago! Things are different now."

"Many things are different. Not everything. Sometimes it takes people a long time to change."

I'll say. Mennonites weren't big on change. We'd only almost lived here since Canada was born and we still had to learn German in school. No wonder people were so surprised when they found out we didn't all still wear long dresses and kerchiefs like the Hutterites.

Mom sighed. "I wanted to make sure my kids learned to speak good English. Now maybe I'm sorry that your father and I didn't speak more German to you when you were little."

"I'm not." I knew enough, maybe not so much as some of my friends did. Mark Giesbrecht and Pete Wiens and Sadie Heppner still spoke Plautdietsch with their parents at home. But mostly the only kids who used German in school were the farm kids like Mark, or the Mexican Mennonite kids. And for sure it wasn't the kind of German you'd use in church.

"Kleenex Krahn called Jillian a *schnoddanaze* at recess. Sadie said it meant know-it-all, but then Mark told us it really meant –"

"*Kleenex* Krahn?" Mom waved the cookie cutter at me.

Oops. "Everyone calls her that."

"It doesn't matter what everyone else does. I don't want you teasing other kids. Understood?"

"Sorry. Anyways, I'm Canadian. Not Dutch or German or Russian or whatever. Shouldn't I learn French if I want to be a good Canadian? Jillian got to take French before she came here."

Mom sighed one of her I-hope-I-won't-be-disappointed-in-you sighs. "*Nah yo*," she said. "There are people, turtles, and three-cornered files."

Which didn't make any sense at all, but was just the kind of thing Mom was all the time saying. "What's that supposed to mean?" I asked.

"It takes all kinds to make a world." Mom turned back to her dough and said something else in Low German that I didn't understand. I got the message, though, so I shut up while I was still ahead yet.

Anyways, the High German we learned in school, and that the old people spoke in church, wasn't anything like the Plautdietsch Mom and Dad used at home. Not to us kids so much, but for sure when my grandparents and aunts and uncles got together, which was pretty much every Sunday, holiday, birthday, and any other old time. Then everyone talked at once. Most of the time it sounded like they were arguing, but then they'd laugh and when I asked them what was so funny they'd chuckle and say, "It's not the same in English."

Plautdietsch was a loud language. My family was a loud family.

But even if we didn't understand most of the words, we kids caught on to a lot more than the grown-ups thought we did.

I didn't need anyone to tell me that my mom and dad had been arguing about me last night, about me and my party that never happened because Mom never felt better all week. Yesterday, the last day of school, she never made it to breakfast even.

When Dad came down in the morning, he'd poured himself a cup of coffee and said, "*Nah, meyahl.* No pajama party in this house tonight. Your mother's not up to it."

"But, Dad!" I protested. "Mom said! She likes my friends to come over. We'll be quiet. I promise. Quiet as mice."

Dad snorted. "Don't make promises you can't keep."

I looked to Beth for help, but she just shook her head at me.

"Everyone's already invited!"

"Then uninvite them," Dad said. "You can have your party another time."

"Isaak, she's been looking forward to this for days already." Mom's soft voice was almost a whisper. She leaned against the doorframe, squinting into the bright kitchen. I felt a sharp pang of guilt at how awful she looked. "I'll be fine," Mom said. "Let her have her party."

I turned back to Dad hopefully, but he never even looked at me. He jumped to his feet and went to help Mom. Even leaning on the doorframe she was wobbling a little, dabbing at the tears in her eyes with a Kleenex.

"Esther, come back to bed." Dad guided Mom out of the room.

As soon as they were gone, Beth got up and stood over me, glaring hard enough to bore a hole through me with her eyes. "You listen and you listen good." She leaned forward, practically in my face. "Leave it alone already."

"It's not fair."

"So what. Life's not fair, in case you hadn't figured that out yet. Think about Mom for once."

Everything was ruined. I had to tell my friends that the party was off. "My Mom's sick," I said.

"What's she got?" asked Sadie.

Only I didn't want to say she had a headache because that sounded like it was nothing, and I couldn't say what she really had because it was too hard to explain. Besides which, I didn't understand it even. So I mumbled something about how it just wasn't going to work out this time.

Jillian said we could all go to her house except her parents planned to be out of town overnight. So then Sadie invited her for a sleepover, and Jillian said she'd ask if she could have a pajama party at her place next weekend. After school let out we all went swimming together like always, but it wasn't the same. For sure it didn't feel like the last day of school is supposed to feel.

At supper I couldn't help it if I was in a bad mood still. Mom shuffled around the kitchen, not looking too good yet, but good enough to fry up some potatoes and hamburgers.

"I'm so sorry, Elsie," she said, stopping a moment to put a cold cloth on the back of her neck.

"It's okay," I muttered. "Never mind." I knew Mom was feeling pretty bad about everything. Only I felt lousy too, and I could feel the waterworks starting up in my eyes. It was too much to try to pretend everything was all right. I got up from the table. "I'm going upstairs to read."

I threw myself on my bed and stared up at the ceiling, wondering how come Sadie hadn't invited me to sleep over, too.

When Lena came to bed later, she told me Mom was crying.

I wished I hadn't been such a brat then, and almost went downstairs to tell her that it really didn't matter that much about the party. Only it was too late already. Mom and Dad were arguing in Plautdietsch. They were arguing about me and my party that never happened.

And then the arguing turned into something else. Mom screamed something at Dad and there was a slap and this loud thud like something had hit the wall or fallen down. I could hear Mom sobbing and I almost got out of bed after all.

After that it was quiet again.

I knew I should pray. I should ask God for forgiveness. I should ask him for his help.

But I was too mad at him right then.

3

What's loose?

Tommy was still waiting to be fed when I got home from my bike ride. I held the porch door open and invited him in, only he wouldn't budge. He never did, no matter what I tried tempting him with. Like he was doing us a favor by letting us feed him.

First thing when I walked in the door, Beth was on my case. "Where did you take off to this morning?" She slammed down the knob on the toaster and glared fiercely at me so I knew pretty much what she was thinking. She was thinking why couldn't I have just kept my mouth shut for once.

"Up yours," I muttered under my breath. I could've said it out loud. It wasn't like Dad was paying attention, sitting there at the kitchen table drinking his coffee like nothing had happened even. And smoking. Mom never

17

would've let him get away with smoking at the table, for sure not while we were eating.

Lena stuffed her grubby fist into a box of Cheerios and then into her mouth. She was wearing my brand-new blue peasant blouse. It figured.

"I don't remember anyone asking to borrow my clothes."

Lena's lower lip pushed out far enough to step on. "It's too small on you, you said so. And blue's my favoritest color. Please?"

"Favorite, not favoritest. You're not a baby." It simply wasn't fair that Lena got the little turned-up pixie nose and I inherited the huge Redekop *gurknaze*. It wasn't fair that Lena got the thick brown hair that tumbled in waves down her back, but my dirty blonde hair was so fine I had to keep it cut short always so I looked almost like a boy. Until this year I didn't mind so much when people thought I was a boy, but now . . .

"Please?" she whined.

"What's the difference, Elsie? Let her wear it this once." Dad butted out his smoke.

"She better not wreck it."

"Go back to bed and get up on the other side, why don't you?" Beth stood at the counter buttering her toast. I stuck my tongue out at her on my way to the fridge. Okay, I was being a brat. I didn't give a care.

"Tommy's hungry. Where's the milk?"

"We're out. You can run to the Co-op and buy some." Beth bit into her toast.

"You go buy it."

"Look, you little ingrate." Toast crumbs spit across the room at me. "I'm in charge until Mom gets home. So you can just smarten up and do what I tell you."

"Say it, don't spray it."

Dad threw us a warning look.

By now my heart was a wild thing. I had to ask. It didn't matter that I already knew. "Where is Mom?"

Dad studied his coffee cup, like the answer might be in there somewheres. "I was just telling Beth and Lena. I took her to the hospital last night."

"You mean Eden. You took her to Eden."

Finally, he looked me in the eye, and now he maybe looked a bit like death warmed over. "*Nah yo*, I mean Eden."

The questions nearly burst out, one after another.

"For how long?"

"Can we visit her?"

"What's wrong with her?"

None of them made it past my tightly pressed lips. I blinked away useless tears. Anyways, I already knew most of the answers.

"A couple of weeks. Maybe a month."

"Not for a few days."

"I wish the hell I knew."

Depression, Dad. It's called depression. I wanted to shout it at him, along with the one question I didn't know the answer to: *Is she ever going to get better?*

All I said was, "I'll go get the damn milk."

"Elsie!" Dad's voice boomed.

Only I was already out the door. I ran across the street, cutting through *Pudel* Pete's yard and the alley to the back entrance of the Co-op.

Eden, Eden, Eden. What kind of *dummkopps* called a mental hospital Eden? Who did they think they were kidding?

This was too big for a wish. I needed serious help.

Dear God, I prayed, ignoring the stones stabbing my bare feet. *I'm sorry, I'm sorry, I'm sorry. I should've kept my mouth shut. I shouldn't have made Mom feel bad about the pajama party. Please make my mother better so she can come home.*

It was a real prayer, not some selfish wish. Okay, maybe a little selfish. But it wasn't like I was praying for bigger boobs or for Aaron Penner to notice me or anything.

Still, God was going to have to work overtime to answer my prayer.

Conditions didn't favor it.

I promise to be good, I added.

Conditions didn't favor that either. I for sure didn't feel like being good.

❧

Grandma Redekop's nose led her across the alley before lunch. She waddled in the back door.

"*Goondach, meyahles.* Oh my, such good girls you are. Doing all the Saturday work." She'd caught us on our knees, Beth scrubbing the kitchen floor and me dusting baseboards in the dining room.

Work was Grandma's answer for most everything. Dad had given us a choice, after I'd got back with the milk. Either Beth was in charge, or he'd ask his mother to come over during the day while he was at work.

"NO!" All three of us had agreed on that much at least. It wasn't that we didn't like Grandma Redekop, or even that she would forcefeed us a steady diet of *plumen mouse hollopchee, varenika,* and borscht. Some of those things I liked even. And Grandma's cooking would for sure be a whole lot better than anything Beth made.

But Grandma would never be done thinking of things to keep us busy. I wouldn't get to spend any time at the pool with my friends if Grandma was in charge.

"Well then," said Dad, running one hand through his Brylcreemed hair like he was ready to tear it out. "Maybe I should phone up your Auntie Nettie or Taunte Tina. One of them could check up on you girls while I'm at work."

Taunte Tina was ancient – all of my mom's sisters were. Dad's sister, Nettie, was my favorite aunt, but she wasn't Mom.

"Dad, I'm sixteen. I can handle it." Beth made a big deal of staring straight at me. "As long as Elsie does her share and helps look after Lena."

"I don't need Elsie to look after me." Lena scowled, folding her arms across her chest. "I'm not a baby!"

"Well, Elsie?" Dad waited.

Like I had a choice. Besides which, I had to do whatever I could to make it up to Mom. "Fine with me."

All my plans for summer got sucked down the drain, just like that. Plans to hang out with my friends, swim, suntan, ride my bike, have pajama parties, and maybe . . . my heart skipped. It was bad luck to even think his name.

None of my plans included taking orders from Beth, or having to *schlap* my little sister along every time I left the house, that's for sure. But it was a good bet that none of Mom's plans included being stuck away in a mental home.

"Good. Then I don't want to hear any more about it." Dad took a cap from the row of hooks by the back door. He faced us again from behind an Elephant Brand fertilizer emblem. "I'm late for work."

On a Saturday? Sure, okay. At the seed plant where my dad worked, he mostly sold seed and fertilizer and stuff to farmers. But seeding was finished weeks ago already so what did he have to work on a Saturday for?

He paused halfway out the door. "Your mom will be just fine in no time, kidlets. Pray for her."

Uy uy uy. Here's the thing. Mom and Beth were the religious ones in our family. Dad was what Reverend Funk would call a backslider. For one thing, he smoked. For another thing, he never hardly went to church. He never hardly said grace before meals, except if Mom made him. And he used words that for sure he didn't find in the Bible.

He was the one telling us to pray? I got a bad feeling in my gut.

I decided to go along with the helping-out bit until lunch. Then I was going to the pool and that was all there was to it. No way was I missing the first Saturday of summer holidays.

"What do I have to –" I started, but there was Beth, hands folded, head bowed and eyes closed yet, before the door even shut behind Dad. Her lips moved silently.

Holy macaroni.

When she finished praying, Beth told me to eat something. "Then we'll clean up the kitchen and make the beds. I guess I should go buy groceries yet, too."

Already it was starting. Before I knew it I was down on my knees with a dust rag. I was still there when Grandma showed up.

"I brought ginger snaps. Isaak's favorite." She never stopped for a breath even. "Tina brought them to me, but who can eat so much? *Vooa es Mutta*? I said I would help this morning with the peas. Now the day is too hot already, not?"

Beth wrung out the floor rag, hard.

Grandma noticed.

"*Vaut es louse, kint*?"

I couldn't help giggling. Plautdietsch was hilarious sometimes. "Me, Grandma. I'm loose." I flopped over like a rag doll. Loose screw. Screw loose.

Grandma didn't laugh. "You make fun of an old woman."

I jumped up and put my arms around her, as far around as I could anyways. "I'm sorry, Grandma. I was just acting silly."

Beth told her what was wrong, scrubbing still harder yet. The kitchen chair groaned as Grandma's bottom spread over both sides. "*Uy uy uy*. So it goes always. And you girls all alone? It's too much. Why did Isaac not make me a phone call?"

"We're fine, Grandma," Beth stood up, pushing a long strand of hair away from her face. "Thanks for the cookies."

Grandma's fingers clasped my wrist like steel handcuffs. She pulled me close. "Come here once, *meyahl*."

She squeezed me against her softness. "Don't worry yourself over it. God will take care of your mother. You'll see. You pray for God to make her well again. God will listen. God always listens."

"I will, Grandma." I wriggled out of her arms.

"You do the best thing you can for your mother, making the house so nice." She nodded her approval. "I'll make the lunch. Throw me over here that apron."

Beth didn't stand a chance.

4

Cottage cheese head

"What kept you?" Jillian asked. She'd saved a spot for me to put my towel beside her. "We waited at Sadie's for ages."

The pool was the best thing about Hopefield. It wasn't anything fancy like the Pan-Am pool in Winnipeg where we'd gone last month on a school field trip. But it was big enough, with two diving boards and lots of grass around the deck where we could tan, and a few trees for shade. Besides which, it was the only place in town for us to hang out except for church or maybe the park.

Sadie lived a block from the pool. We usually met at her house after lunch – Jillian and me – and sometimes Naomi, Joy, Heather, and Eleanor, too.

"My grandma was over," I said, dodging the question. I didn't feel like explaining about Mom right then. Maybe if it was just Jillian I'd have said something, but not with everyone there, the guys yet, too. Caleb, Pete, Mark, Jimmy, Richard. And Aaron. Especially Aaron Penner.

For now I just wanted to have some fun. First thing, we split into teams – girls against guys – to dive for pennies. There were no rules. Anything went.

"Ready?" Naomi tossed a penny into the middle of the deep end.

We took turns, three people from each team diving at once. Sadie, Jillian, and I stood at the edge, ready to dive against Pete, Mark, and Aaron.

"Set."

We watched the penny sink to the bottom.

"Go!"

We hit the water, kicking like crazy. I'd got a good start, and guessed that the penny probably slid down the slope to the deepest part of the pool. There it was, skittering along the bottom. I grabbed it and kicked off the bottom, heading for the side of the pool.

"Got it!" I slammed the penny down on the concrete, a split second before Aaron yanked me under.

I whipped around underwater, grinning, showing him my empty hands. Our laughs gurgled up to the surface with us. "Slowpoke," I mocked.

"You won't be so lucky next time."

"Hah!" My wrist tingled where Aaron had held it.

He got a better start than I did on our next turn, so I tried to force him off course. Only someone's hand clamped around my ankle and held me back. Mark. He wrapped both arms around my leg.

I kicked out hard, but he had a pretty good grip. I couldn't hold my breath much longer. I started to panic, twisting around to kick out at Mark's stomach with my free leg. He was lucky I didn't aim lower. Finally he let go and I scrambled for the surface, gasping for air.

"What're you trying to do, you retard? Drown me?"

"Wimp." Mark splashed me as he swam by. "*Schmocke bayn*. Nice legs. Don't you ever shave them? I'll lend you a swather and baler."

I was too stunned to put my brain into gear. If only I'd hurled an insult right back at him everything would have been all right.

"*Fuy*," I scowled like an old woman, then dove underwater to cool my flaming face, hating Mark Giesbrecht with every ounce of my soul and not caring one iota if God knew exactly how I felt, even if it was a sin.

Did the others hear him, I wondered? Did –? Oh, John Jacob Jingleheimer. Exhaling, I let myself sink to the bottom of the pool. When Aaron had dunked me before – did he think my legs were hairy, too?

Eventually I had to swim back and pretend nothing had happened. The fun had gone out of the game, though. I stopped even trying, then we had to quit because the lifeguards blew their whistles for a pool check.

The others stretched out on the grass to suntan, but I wanted to stay as far away from Mark as possible. I went to find Lena, and Jillian came with. When the lifeguards finished checking the pool, we ducked into the shallow end to horse around a bit, letting Lena and her friends swim between our legs and dive off our shoulders. Then we knelt in the shallowest water and watched the little kids.

"Don't pay any attention to Mark," Jillian said. "He's a *glommskopp*."

So she had heard. "Do you even know what that means?"

"Pete told me. Idiot or blockhead or something like that."

"Close enough. It means cottage cheese head."

She giggled. "How perfect is that? *Glommskopp*."

"Uh-huh." I had to smile a little because now Jillian had a new favorite Plautdietsch word. I ducked underwater, coming up again with my head tipped back so the water smoothed my hair. "Did the others hear, too?"

Jillian shrugged. "Don't worry about it."

"Do you shave your legs?" I asked, quickly, before I lost my nerve. Really, when you think about it, whether a person shaves their legs or not is nobody else's business.

Jillian grinned. "Not because I want to. But one time I borrowed my mom's razor and tried it. And then the hair grew back and was so prickly I couldn't stand it. I couldn't even sleep at night. So now I have to shave practically every week."

"What did your mom say?"

"She said I was far too young to worry about a little hair on my legs, and it was my own fault for using her things without asking. But she bought me my own razor. Why don't you ask your mom to get you one?"

"Yeah, I probably will," I lied. I was beginning to see what Reverend Funk meant when he said one lie just led to another.

After a while we joined the others. I made sure to stretch out with my feet against the fence, so no one would be forced to look at my gross hairy legs.

When the pool closed I looked for Lena. Only she was gone already. And so was her bike.

"She's probably at home," Jillian said.

"She'd better be," I muttered.

We rode home together like always, the bunch of us, hogging most of the road until we had to move over for some guy in an old brown pick-up, driving right on our tail. He crawled by, giving us the evil eye, but we all pretty much ignored him.

Pete turned off at Jillian's street with her. I was a little jealous, even though we all knew Pete had had a crush on Jillian since that day she walked into our grade 3 class with her six-shooters on.

Sure enough, Lena's bike was leaning against the porch when I got home. *Thank you, God.* From the back alley already I could hear Beth having a spaz.

"She never listens, Dad. What if some pervert had walked off with Lena?"

As if that would happen, I thought. This was Hopefield, for Pete's sake. There *were* no strangers. Besides, Lena

was almost eight already. She knew better than to go off
with someone she didn't know. So how come I felt so
relieved that she was home safe?

"I'll talk to her," Dad's voice rumbled.

"I hope you ground her at least."

That did it. Beth was doing her level best to get me in
trouble. I stomped into the house. "You don't have to be
such a worrywart. Lena's home, isn't she?" I was a bit surprised to see Auntie Nettie sitting there with Dad.
Grandma must've told her about Mom already. I gave her
a quick nod.

"No thanks to you. You're supposed to be watching
her!" Beth practically spit in my face.

"I was watching her!" I shouted right back. "I played
with her even. I can't keep my eyes on her every second.
There are lifeguards at the pool, you know."

"That's not the point!"

"Well, what is the point? It's not like Lena doesn't
know the way home!"

I waited for Beth to spout off some more, but instead,
Dad jumped in.

"Lena got back an hour ago." He was pretty steamed.
"Not only did she ride home alone, she's burned to a
crisp."

Rats. "Can I help it if she takes off without telling
me?"

Beth snorted, but Dad glared at her from under his
bushy eyebrows and she kept her big yap shut for once.

"I expect better from you, Elsie," he said. "I have to be able to count on you to keep track of your little sister. Especially now, while Mom's away. Lena shouldn't be gallivanting around town without anyone knowing where she is."

There wasn't anything more I could say, which didn't stop blabbermouth me from saying it. "So I'm supposed to let her just tag along everywhere with me and my friends. That's not fair!"

As soon as the words were out of my mouth, I knew I'd said one thing too many. The wrath of Dad was about to descend.

"Who said anything about fair!" he bellowed.

Auntie Nettie rose quietly. She brushed her hand against Dad's shoulder as she walked by him to the sink.

His eyes followed her and he sighed. "No swimming for either of you until Lena's sunburn heals. Now go check if she's okay and call her to eat. Nettie brought over supper for us."

"Thanks, Auntie Nettie," I muttered, but never moved, just glared at Dad like I was daring him to completely blow his stack.

"And if it happens again," Dad's voice rose, "you won't be going to the pool at all for the rest of the summer! Now SCRAM! VAMOOSE!"

I scurried by him and up the stairs, slamming the bedroom door shut. As if Dad would ground me from swimming for the whole summer.

Our room was darkened, the blinds pulled. Lena lay on her stomach, whimpering. I grabbed the Noxzema from the dresser and sat beside her on the bed.

"Don't touch me!"

"This goop will cool you off." Feeling the heat rise off her skin took away some of the mad inside me. Maybe I had screwed up, but Beth made it sound a lot worse than it was, talking about perverts yet. I mean, Hopefield might have its share of weirdos, but not like that.

"Owww!"

"Hold still." I tried to be more gentle. "Thanks for taking off without telling me. Now I can't go swimming." Mom wouldn't have grounded me. She wouldn't have yelled at me either. She wouldn't have even told Dad that Lena had come home alone.

"I went to Jessie's for a Popsicle. I couldn't find you."

"You couldn't have looked too hard."

There was a soft knock and Auntie Nettie opened the door. She was holding a glass of water. "For Lena. She should drink."

Lena gulped it down obediently while Auntie Nettie felt her forehead and back. "You are burning up, *meyahl*."

Auntie Nettie didn't say anything about me letting everyone down, but somehow I felt worse than before. She helped me smear more cream on Lena's neck, back, and arms. The tops of her legs and backs of her knees were pretty bad, too. When her skin was coated we got her into a baggy T-shirt that hung down to her knees.

"Supper's ready. C'mon." I gathered our wet towels and bathing suits to hang up outside.

"Sorry you got in trouble." Lena held her arms out from her sides and shuffled out of the room, trying not to bend her elbows or knees, wincing with every step.

She actually looked pretty funny, but I knew it wouldn't be too smart to laugh. "And I'm sorry you got so burned," I sighed.

"Not to worry. Everyone makes mistakes. How else do we learn?" Auntie Nettie squeezed my shoulders. "Come. You'll feel better after you eat."

Even with more Noxzema before bedtime, Lena whimpered most of the night.

She wasn't the only one I'd forgotten about either. I'd hardly thought about Mom the whole afternoon. What kind of daughter was I, anyways?

❧

Dear God,

I didn't mean to forget about Lena today. I was just having fun. Then that glommskopp Mark Giesbrecht . . . well, you know what happened. I'm sorry, and I'm sorry about lying to Jillian and for feeling jealous because Pete likes her and Aaron doesn't even know I'm alive. I'm not sorry for thinking Mark is a moron because he is, but I'll try to stop hating him. Maybe you could help me figure out a way to get him to stop bugging me so much all the time.

I'm a little bit sorry about mouthing off to Dad, but he should be sorry too, for yelling at me. How come he has to be so grouchy all the time?

I don't understand about Mom. I know she was upset and everything, over all the fuss I made about the pajama party. But I don't understand how someone can get so sad they have to go to a hospital. I don't understand why you let her get sick again. You must have a reason. Maybe this is a test, like the one you gave Jonah when he was swallowed by the whale. I'll try hard to have faith in you. I promise to do what Dad and Beth say, and help out around the house and take care of Lena and everything. I promise to try my hardest, only please, make Mom better.

And if you don't mind, please hurry. It's summer.

Amen.

5

Children's questions sprinkled with sugar

At church the next morning, Reverend Funk called out the names of all the sick people. He called out my mom's name, too, Esther Redekop, and asked the congregation to pray for her. So then everyone knew. *Nah yo.* So it goes always, not?

When Lena and I walked in the door, Dad was already on the phone. "No. We're managing pretty well, thank you. The girls are all pitching in." He rolled his eyes at us. "Yes, thank you, Mrs. Koehler. Bye now."

Dad groaned. "Just what I need. The whole church traipsing down here to stick their noses in our business."

"You should be happy so many people will be praying for Mom." Beth tied an apron around her waist and went to stir the pot she'd left simmering on the stove.

Now seemed like a good time to change the subject. "I'm hungry, what's for dinner?" I tried peeking into the pot.

Beth shooed me away. "Children's questions sprinkled with sugar," she said, all sweet and sappy. Like she was trying to sound like Mom, using one of her lines and everything.

"Don't even bother," I said.

Beth started to snap back at me and then she bit her tongue. She looked a little hurt maybe, but what was she trying to prove anyways?

By the time we sat down to eat, I really, truly was starving. Auntie Nettie had brought *summaborscht* for supper last night. *Fuy* and double *fuy*. I'd barely touched mine, filling up on fresh brown bread instead. Only thing was, man could not live by bread alone, even if it was home-made. And instead of pancakes this morning, all we got was cereal. A bowl of cereal wasn't enough to get a person through one of Reverend Funk's sermons.

This morning he'd talked about Daniel, and how Daniel had spent twenty-one days praying in order to come to know the will of God. He didn't eat any bread or meat, or drink any wine the whole time. At the end of twenty-one days, God appeared to Daniel in a vision, and Daniel fell on the ground before him. Then God touched Daniel and gave him strength. Reverend Funk said the same thing can happen in the lives of Christians today. Then we sang, "Dare to be a Daniel."

"Stew?" I turned up my nose at the slop on my plate. "We're having stew?"

"What's your problem?" Beth was standing there with a ladle of goop. She looked like she had a good idea of what she'd like to do with it, too.

"Nothing, only –" I bit my lip. I'd said the wrong thing. Again. After I'd promised God and everything. "Sundays we usually have chicken, that's all." Roast chicken with *bubbat*, which Mom said was Mennonite dressing, but which was really more like cake with raisins in it. Yummy. And mashed potatoes and gravy and peas. My stomach growled just thinking about it.

"Well, this Sunday we're having stew. If that's not good enough for you, too bad."

"It's good enough." I put a piece of meat in my mouth and started chewing, to show her.

"I'll have you know that I missed Sunday School and was late for church so I could make this stew." Beth was snarly even for Beth.

All I could do was smile and nod, since I was chewing still.

"There are plenty of people in this world who are starving, you know, people who would be only too glad to have a hot bowl of stew."

Now she really did sound like Mom. Still chewing, I mumbled. "I know." Never mind that it was 80° outside.

"They can have mine," said Lena, pushing her food away. She crossed her arms and frowned so hard her eyebrows nearly touched. I knew that look.

Dad obviously didn't, or else he wasn't paying attention again. "Do you girls always have to natter at each
other? Eat your dinner."

I could have told him that wasn't going to work. Only
I was still chewing yet.

Tears flooded Lena's eyes. "I can't. It tastes like, like . . ."
She looked to me.

I managed to swallow. "Like crud?"

"Yeah. Like crud."

Now Beth got all blurry-eyed and red-faced. "I don't
know why I bother."

"Have you tasted it?" I asked her.

By now Dad had sampled the stew for himself. "Maybe
we should go out to eat. It is Sunday. Stew is always better
the second day."

"*Oooo!*" Beth pushed back her chair and began banging
dishes around.

"*Oooo!*" I was pretty good at imitating Beth. Lena
giggled.

Soap suds flew across the room as Beth whipped around.
"You're such an imbecile!"

"What's an imbecile?" asked Lena.

"It's a fancy word for idiot," I explained. I knew a lot
of words my friends didn't know. For one thing I read a
lot. But I also made a point of looking up any word Beth
used to insult me with.

"Oh. Why doesn't she say idiot then?"

"She thinks I'm too stupid to know I've been insulted and that's like, you know, a super-duper insult." I grinned widely, teeth and everything.

"Enough!" Dad slammed his fist on the table. A fork jumped to the floor. He barked out something in Plautdietsch.

He didn't need to translate. We all buttoned our lips. In the end we went out to the Harvester for burgers, and then Dad said he was going to see Mom.

"Can we come with?" Lena asked.

"Not today."

So Lena gave him a card she'd made for Mom. I gave him the notes I'd taken in church so Mom wouldn't miss the sermon about Daniel.

Tommy meowed loudly when Dad dropped us off at home. He scowled and shoved the cat out of his way with his foot. "If no one is going to feed that animal, I'm going to get rid of it. Some farmer would take it for his barn."

"Don't look at me," Beth said. "I've got enough to do without worrying about a grungy old alley cat yet."

"I'll feed him," I told Dad.

Please God, give me strength.

❧

After Dad left, Beth said she had a headache and went to have a lie-down. Lena disappeared next door to play with a friend. I filled Tommy's saucer with milk and made some frozen Kool-Aid pops for later. Then I changed into my bathing suit, grabbed a book and a glass of left-over Kool-Aid, and went to lie in the sun. If I couldn't go swimming, I could at least work on my tan.

I was rubbing lotion on my hairy legs when the light-bulb went on upstairs. Now was the perfect time to experiment. Beth kept her stuff in a bathroom drawer; she probably had a razor or some of that hair removal guck in there. I would try both, I decided, to see which did a better job.

The house was dead quiet as I tiptoed across the kitchen. I pushed open the bathroom door slowly so it wouldn't creak and give me away, opening it just enough to slip inside. I didn't see Beth standing there in her house-coat until it was too late already. She had one foot propped on the toilet lid, and was using a wad of toilet paper to wipe at a trickle of blood running down her bare leg.

At first I was too stunned to move. Then Beth looked up and saw me. You can bet I moved pretty quick then, fumbling for the door knob behind my back.

"Get out of here you little brat!"

Opening the door, I backed out. "Are you okay?"

Beth's face was so red and twisted I thought she was maybe going to explode. She reached for a bar of soap. "GET OUT!"

I ducked, pulling the door shut. The soap thudded against the other side. "At least now I know why you've been in such a crappy mood!" I shouted at the closed door. Then I made a beeline outside.

Man-a-livin' anyways, if she didn't want someone to walk in on her, she should've locked the stupid door. Still, I was pretty embarrassed. I picked up Tommy to cuddle. Beth wasn't hurt. She just had her period. That didn't take much to figure out. Only who knew a person could bleed like that? I mean, we'd seen the film and had the talk in school and everything, but that kind of detail had never come up. I'd sort of imagined it would be like a leaky faucet. A drip here, a drip there. Not an actual trickle.

So far Naomi was the only one I knew who'd started already. On the first day the pool opened we'd all gone swimming only Naomi said she couldn't go because of "you-know-what" and you bet we all knew exactly what "what" was. I'd made up my mind right then that there was no way I was going to miss out on swimming because of some stupid period. I'd use those tampon things instead of pads – that's all there was to it.

Tommy wriggled out of my arms and I remembered to breathe.

What if it happened this summer? I wasn't ready. No way could I ask Dad to buy me what I needed. He wouldn't have the foggiest clue. No way could I buy what I needed myself. Even if I could stand the embarrassment, I'd seen the boxes lining the shelves at Rexall Drugs. Regular, super, super plus, ultra super. How was I supposed to know which one to buy? What if someone I knew walked into the store when I was paying for it? What if there was a *boy* at the cash register that day?

After what just happened, I didn't think it would be a good idea to ask Beth to help me. Not until she cooled off, that was for sure. Which wasn't going to be any time soon, judging by the look on her face.

This wasn't the sort of problem I wanted to talk to God about either, though it was sort of his fault. I mean, He was the one who made us the way we were and everything.

I had little choice, really. I'd have to swipe what I needed from Beth. God would understand. I hoped.

Sweat poured off me so I moved into the shade, not daring to go back inside. A good hour later Beth stuck her head out and told me to go fetch Lena from next door. "Dad will be home soon. Auntie Nettie phoned and invited us for *faspa*."

For once I didn't argue. *Faspa* at Auntie Nettie's was always more than the usual coffee, buns, and cheese. There'd be homemade sausage and meat pies, probably plum *platz* and chokecherry *piroshki*, and for sure one of her famous chocolate cakes.

Only Lena had other ideas. She wouldn't budge from the neighbor's porch. "I'm staying here. We're making a play."

"You can come back later. Say good-bye."

"Good-bye," Lena said smugly, and turned on her heel to go back inside. I didn't have the patience today for her games. So I grabbed her around the waist and carried her across the yard, kicking and screaming.

"*Owww!* You're hurting me!"

Honest, until that second I'd forgotten all about her sunburn. As soon as I put her down her teeth clamped on my arm.

"Ouch!" I let go. "You bit me!" Lena scooted off. Sunburn or not, no way was she getting away with that. I chased her down, grabbing her wrist and trying not to touch her anywhere else as I dragged her home. She dug in her heels and fought me every step of the way, bawling like all get out.

Beth came tearing out of the house, screaming at me to smarten up. I was too busy trying to hang on to Lena to listen. Next thing I knew Beth had me in a headlock, so I kicked her in the shins. Somehow my fingers got all tangled up in her hair. All the while Lena was trying to get my other hand close enough to her mouth to bite me again.

Right about then I saw someone out of the corner of my eye. It was Reverend Funk and Mrs. Funk, coming up the walk.

Next thing I heard a car door slam behind the house. My brain put two and two together and figured out Dad was home. Only problem was the message took a second to get from my brain to the rest of me.

"WHAT IN BLAZES?!"

Message received. I did the only thing I could think to do. I let go of Lena.

Lena toppled straight back, right into Mrs. Funk. Mrs. Funk stumbled backward, too. Only the heel of her shoe somehow got wedged in a crack in the sidewalk. I have to admit, she tried her best to recover her balance without dropping the coffee cake she was carrying.

Too bad Mrs. Funk was a little bottom-heavy. She went down hard. She landed on her bum in the flowerbed, one shoe on and one shoe off, right on top of Mom's forget-me-nots.

The coffee cake landed in her lap, upside down.

Lena landed on the coffee cake.

"In the house," Dad choked, his face scarlet. "Scoot!"

The three of us practically left skid marks, we scooted so fast. Into the house and straight to our rooms.

6

Too many weeds in the garden

When I was five years old a crusade came to Hopefield. The evangelist thundering from our church pulpit put the fear of the Lord into me. That night I knelt beside my mother and asked God to forgive my sins. I accepted the Lord Jesus Christ as my savior and was born again.

I don't remember what sort of sins I'd committed when I was five. Probably I fought with Beth. Probably it wasn't any different back when I was five than it is now.

All I remember is being terrified that I was going to burn in hell for eternity.

Anyways, that time when I was five didn't really count, because after you repent and are saved you're supposed to get baptized, to let other people know you're serious about it. Beth says people can only get baptized in a Mennonite church if they're old enough to understand what it all means, like to be a Christian and become a

45

church member and everything. It's because Mennonites are Anabaptists. It's a big deal. In the olden days, the first Anabaptists were burned at the stake and everything.

Beth took baptism classes and got baptized last year and has been a royal pain in the behind ever since. Excuse me, but it's true. First she gave her testimony in church, all about the day Jesus saved her. Then on baptism Sunday, she stepped into the pool that was up high behind the choir pews. Usually it was hidden behind a panel of some kind. But on baptism Sundays the panel came off and there was the pool with Reverend Funk, all in white, standing in water up to his waist. The pool was really more like a big tub, but a mural on the wall behind was supposed to make it look like the reverend was standing in a river. It all looked pretty fake, if you ask me.

The baptism candidates – that's what they're called – they wore white robes. A floodlight shone on the pool and the congregation sang, "Shall We Gather at the River."

Even though the mural and everything seemed fake, when everyone started singing, it was hard not to get all choked up and shivery. You really felt religious then. You almost wanted to be up there getting baptized yourself so you would maybe always have that kind of feeling.

When Beth was in the water Reverend Funk put one hand on her back. With his other hand he held her hands folded over her chest. He said, "Do you confess your sins and accept Jesus Christ as your personal savior?"

And Beth said "I do."

It was like she was marrying God.

The reverend dunked her backwards into the water and pulled her up again. She climbed soaking wet out of the pool with her gown clinging to her so there wasn't much left to the imagination, that was for sure.

"Did you get water up your nose?" I asked Beth later. I always got water up my nose when I got dunked backwards.

"Do you have to act so infantile?" she said.

I didn't think that was such a Christian thing to say.

At the MB church they dunked you all the way under. My friend Heather told me that at the Bergthaler Mennonite church where she went, they only sprinkled water over your head. It made me wonder how they baptized people at the five other Mennonite churches in town.

We'd gone to the MB for as long as I could remember, at least Mom, Beth, Lena, and I had. We always sat in the back pew, because sometimes Dad would sneak in after the service had started already and sit with us. I liked it when Dad came to church because he gave us Life Savers when Reverend Funk got too long winded, which was pretty much every Sunday.

Besides Sunday School and church service on Sundays, I went to Pioneer Girls on Wednesday evenings and junior choir practice Friday nights. Soon I'd be old enough to start Young People's on Sunday nights, too.

Mom told me once that we went to the MB because they had a service in English and not just German. And because Reverend Thiessen who used to be the reverend there was the only one who would marry them after Dad joined the Air Force when Canada went to war against Hitler. See, if you belong to the Mennonite church you're not supposed to fight or kill other people, no matter what. Mennonites are pacifists. They believe Christians are supposed to follow Christ's example and turn the other cheek, love their enemies, and do good to those who hate them. They're supposed to be peacemakers, not soldiers.

I'm not much of a peacemaker, but then just because our parents and grandparents and great-grandparents were Mennonites, doesn't mean that I'm a Mennonite. No one is really a Mennonite until they are baptized. That's what *schnoddanaze* Beth says. It doesn't matter how much *kielke* or *plumen mouse* you eat.

"Even Mennonites can't agree on what being a Mennonite means," my mom says.

One of the main reasons Mennonites came to Canada was to get away from the fighting in Russia, and because in Canada they wouldn't have to join the army. It was the same reason they'd moved to Russia in the first place, because Catherine the Great promised pretty much the same thing about a hundred years earlier yet.

Mennonites always wandered around a lot, I guess. They wanted to stay separate from the rest of the world.

Anyways, my dad says there wasn't really any place in the world you could go to get away from war anymore.

Even right now here in Canada we're smack in between the United States and the Soviets. Who knows when the

Cold War might warm up and one of them will launch a missile over the north pole and it could come flying over our heads or maybe go off course and *KABOOM!* That would be the end of that because a nuclear bomb incinerates everything. Most of the time I tried not to think about it but sometimes at night it was hard not to.

My dad didn't kill anyone in the war. He joined the ground crew and learned to be a mechanic that fixed plane engines. But then he never left Canada even because he got sick with rheumatic fever and the Air Force sent him home.

The Bergthaler Mennonite Church where my dad was baptized when he was a teenager said working on the engines so the planes could go off and kill people was the same as killing people. They said he should have done alternative service, like in the forestry camps or the coal mines.

"Where is the difference?" my dad asked. Didn't the army use coal? Didn't soldiers keep the country safe so Mennonites could plant trees and go to church? Didn't Mennonites all the time join up as medics who fixed up the soldiers so they could fight another day?

But the church said that if Isaak Redekop – that's my dad – wanted to marry Esther Hiebert – that's my mom – in their church, he would have to get up in front of the congregation and confess his sin and ask for forgiveness.

"*Vite dee,*" my dad said. Which in Plautdietsch means "know yourself," but which really means "mind your own beeswax," only not so polite.

So Mom and Dad got married in the MB instead. Reverend Thiessen didn't see things the same way, I guess. Good thing there are seven Mennonite churches in Hopefield or maybe my parents wouldn't have found one to marry them and then I wouldn't be here.

Anyways, I'm not five anymore. I don't think that being scared to death of hell is a good reason to believe in heaven. But even now I've turned twelve already, I don't understand it all. Like why does God let people in poor countries starve or let people blow each other up in wars or make floods that drown all the crops?

Or take my mother away.

This wasn't the first time Mom had been gone. It wasn't the second time either. Maybe it was the third or fourth time. I don't know for sure. I tried not to remember about those times.

How many more times was God going to take her away? Maybe I was doing something wrong. Maybe God was punishing me for my sins – for how I made a stink when Dad said the pajama party was canceled instead of right away honoring my father and mother like it says in the ten commandments.

Mom had been gone two days. So far I'd let Lena get sunburned, walked in on Beth, lied to my best friend, fought with my sisters, knocked the Reverend's wife over, and totally humiliated my father. Probably I'd set some kind of new record. No wonder Mom had to get away from here; I wanted to get away from me, too.

For sure there were a lot of weeds growing in my garden.

~

A knock on the door woke me up. The light in the room told me I'd slept away the afternoon, and my stomach told me I'd missed *faspa* yet, too. Dad came in and sat on the edge of my bed.

"How would you like a job painting?" he said. Just like that. Out of the blue.

I rubbed my eyes and sat up. "Huh? Me?"

Dad looked a bit desperate. "I'll hire you to paint the garage."

Mornings only, he said. I'd still have to take Lena to the pool with me in the afternoons. But he'd pay me, a dollar an hour, to scrape, sand, prime, and paint the siding and trim on the garage.

Probably I looked as confused as I felt.

"Things can't go on like this all summer or you girls will end up killing each other," Dad said. "Or someone else."

All summer? Did he think Mom might be away all summer?

"Actually," he admitted, "it was Nettie's idea. She thought you needed a project to keep you busy. There's some chocolate cake in the kitchen that she sent home for you, too."

Good ol' Auntie Nettie.

I decided to take the job. It would be one way I could make it up to Mom, to surprise her when she came home. And it would show Dad *and* God that I was really trying to be a good daughter and a good Christian. Plus I could use the money to buy myself a new bike and I'd get a really great tan and Beth wouldn't be able to tell me what to do because I'd be the boss.

I also decided to pray to God for twenty-one days, like Daniel. Then maybe I'd understand Him better. It wouldn't be hard to stay away from wine, since I didn't drink it anyways. If Beth's cooking didn't improve, giving up meat wouldn't be a great hardship either. Not eating any bread might be a problem, but I'd cross that bridge when I came to it.

Twenty-one days was three weeks. Lots of time for God to make my mother well again. Summer holidays would be more than half over already.

I wondered if I would have a vision.

❧

Dear God,

    Please forgive me for fighting with Beth and Lena, and for what happened to Mrs. Funk and for embarrassing Dad and everything.

    I solemnly promise to pray to you every day for twenty-one days. And I promise not to eat any meat or bread or drink any wine either, so that my heart, mind, and body will be clear and open to understanding your will, just like Daniel.

I wondered if I should pray in any special way. Should I close my eyes and bow my head and kneel down, or should I just pray anywhere and anytime in my head, which was the everyday kind of praying. I decided I would pray at bedtime, because then I wouldn't forget, but I would talk to God inside my head, or else Lena would wonder what I was doing on my knees all the time and she'd tell Beth and then Beth would think she'd made some kind of convert and I was going to be a holy roller like her yet.

I pray it is your will to make my mother well again so she can come home. Please help me to do a good job of painting the garage.

Amen.

1

On two legs like a gander

First thing after breakfast on Monday Dad made us go apologize to Reverend Funk and Mrs. Funk. They were pretty forgiving. Being who they were, they sort of had to be. I mean, forgiving others their trespasses is in the Lord's Prayer and everything; it's practically a commandment.

At first I think they were surprised to see us but Reverend Funk invited us in all the same. "How's it going?" he asked.

I almost blurted, "On two legs, like a gander," which is what Dad said all the time when someone asked him how it was going. I bit my tongue just in time, but I had to cover my mouth with my hand to keep the giggles inside.

"Fine, thank you," said Beth. We weren't even in the house yet and she was giving me a dirty look. She handed

Mrs. Funk the coffee cake we'd made. "This is for you. We're terribly sorry about what happened."

"Beth baked the cake," added Lena. "And me and Elsie made the icing."

"You mean, 'Elsie and I made the icing,'" Beth corrected her. Beth was all the time trying to make us speak English properly so we wouldn't sound like country bumpkins. She had her work cut out for her.

"No you didn't," said Lena. "Me and Elsie did."

Reverend Funk had a good chuckle. Beth should've known better than to try and make us look good.

Mrs. Funk held the cake out in front of her like it might jump into her lap or explode or something.

"How nice." She smiled at Lena. "I'll just put this in the kitchen."

I'd never been in the home of a man of God before. There wasn't a thing out of place in the Funk's house. Not a speck of dust. The vacuum lines in the carpet didn't cross each other even.

Immaculate was a good word to describe the living room. For sure the rest of the house was the same. Like the Funks were maybe expecting Jesus to pop in for a visit. All ready for the second coming.

I perched on the edge of the sofa so I wouldn't get the cushion dirty, and tried to tuck my bare feet out of sight and not squirm too much. At first I worried Mrs. Funk would offer us a piece of Beth's coffee cake. No matter how careful I was I knew I'd leave crumbs all over her spotless carpet. But she never offered, which was a relief.

"We won't stay long. We just stopped by to apologize." Beth nodded at me.

I cleared my throat. I'd practiced what to say on the way over. "I'm sorry I was fighting with Lena and that we crashed into you. It was a dreadful accident." Beth had told me to leave out the "dreadful" part, but I thought it was just the right word for the occasion. Anyways, who knew when I'd get to use it again?

"And I'm sorry I fell on top of you," Lena said. "I didn't mean to."

"We hope you weren't hurt." I added that bit because I thought it helped show how sorry we were, even though Mrs. Funk couldn't really be hurt since the flower bed was pretty soft and Lena was still small yet.

"Apology accepted," Mrs. Funk sniffed.

Reverend Funk thanked us. He said he thought we'd all learned a valuable lesson about working out our differences and respecting each other's feelings, rather than resorting to physical force. "Demonstrating Christ's love in our daily lives begins within our own families."

"Would you lead us in asking for God's forgiveness?" asked Beth.

Holy Moses. If you ask me she was laying it on a little thick. Besides which, I'd already prayed for God's forgiveness on my own. But no one asked me, and Reverend

Funk was sure glad to be asked. Before I knew it there we were, kneeling in the Funk's immaculate living room. The reverend put one hand on my head and the other one on Lena's.

"'Create in me a clean heart, O God; and renew a right spirit within me,'" he prayed. I bowed my head. With his hand on it there wasn't much else I could do. I kept my mouth shut and tried to listen to what he was saying, but all the time I was thinking that I wanted to get the heck out of there. I knew I should feel close to God and everything, but I guess there was something wrong with me because I didn't. I felt about as far away from God as a person could get. My neck hurt by the time Reverend Funk said, "Amen."

"It must be hard for you girls with no mother at home," Mrs. Funk said, smiling a tight little smile. "I can understand how you might have trouble coping, Beth, with so much responsibility for the house and your rather, uh, rambunctious younger sisters."

It wasn't like she'd said anything we didn't know already. But the way she said it, talking down her nose like, made it sound like Lena and I were beetles of some kind. The rambunctious dungbugs. I wanted to crawl under the sofa. Except probably it was so clean under there I wouldn't be able to find any dirt to hang out with.

"Elsie and Lena help quite a lot with the housework. Elsie is even painting the garage," said Beth.

"Really." Mrs. Funk raised one eyebrow at me.

I was so stunned by what Beth said I forgot to be insulted by Mrs. Funk's eyebrow. I even grinned a little. Beth's cheeks were turning a real nice shade of pink, but she sat with her back stiff and her chin in the air. Wonders never cease, my mom says.

When we left, Reverend Funk said he'd be sure to remember our mother in his prayers. "Take comfort in knowing He is with you. Leave your troubles in the hands of God."

One thing for sure, with all the praying going on for Mom, sooner or later God was going to have to do something.

"Well," said Beth, as soon as we were out the door, "that went pretty well, don't you think?"

I was so glad to be outside breathing fresh air I could've hugged her. I lifted my face and arms up to the blue sky and felt the warm sunshine soaking through to my cold bones. "It went on two legs like a gander," I said.

Beth sighed. "Reprobate."

I didn't have a clue what she meant, and even though I knew it couldn't be anything good, I decided to let it go because of the way Beth stuck up for me with Mrs. Funk. But I made a mental note to look up *reprobate* in the dictionary.

"If they come to visit us again I'm hiding," said Lena.

I'd bet my last nickel that the reverend and his wife

wouldn't come anywhere near our place for a long time. "C'mon," I said. "I'll race you home."

We ran all the way. Beth and I let Lena win.

∼

Dear God,

I started my new job today, since I was still grounded yet. Only I didn't get to paint. Before I can paint there's a lot of other stuff to do. Today I swept and hosed all the dirt and spider webs off the garage. When Lena came out to watch I hosed her off, too. She liked it. At least she kept coming back for more until Beth told us to quit goofing off.

I'm a little hungry because I didn't eat any meat or bread all day, not even one of the fresh cinnamon buns Grandma baked. Don't get me wrong – I'm not complaining. I just wanted you to know. Anyways, I didn't miss much. Supper was leftover stew. I only ate the vegetables.

Beth didn't notice that I snooped through her drawers and swiped some of her things. You know what I mean. I found a little instruction sheet in the box. It has pictures and every-thing, so I think I'll be okay when the time comes. I'm sorry for taking them without asking. I didn't know what else to do. I promise to replace her stuff as soon as I can.

We apologized to the Funks today. I guess you know that. Reverend Funk said to leave our troubles in God's hands. Sometimes I wonder how your hands can hold all the bad things in the world. Sometimes I wonder if my mother being sick is so small a problem compared to all the other problems in the world that it might slip out between your fingers.

I'm sorry, God. Please cleanse my heart from doubt and other sins, like the reverend said. I know you'll do what's best for my mother. Please help me understand your will.

Amen.

8

Lying has short legs

"I'm thinking about becoming a vegetarian," I told Dad and Beth at lunch the next day, "so I'll need some stuff from the grocery store." Grandma was there, too. She'd come over because she said our windows needed a good washing.

I'd written out a list: nuts, macaroni and cheese, pork and beans (without the pork), fruit, yogurt, ice cream, chocolate bars – stuff like that. We had lots of vegetables in the garden already, so I didn't need to put any on the list.

"Think again," Beth said, handing the list back.

"Daaad."

"Don't be silly, Elsie. Eat your lunch." He didn't look up from his newspaper even.

Lunch was Klik and lettuce bunwiches with carrot sticks and the leftover chocolate cake from Auntie Nettie. I took the lettuce out of the sandwich. "I told you, I'm giving up meat for a while. Bread, too." The piece of limp lettuce didn't look all that appetizing, but I chomped down on it to make a point.

Beth snorted. "Since when?"

I ignored her. "This is all healthy stuff. Mostly, anyways. See, Dad?" I shoved the list in front of his nose. "Don't you want me to eat healthy? Especially when I'm working so hard?" I was working hard. I'd used the wire brush Dad had given me to scrape loose paint off the garage siding all morning.

"How did you get a cockamamie idea like this in your head?" Dad sighed.

I shrugged, wondering what to say that wouldn't be a lie exactly. "I want to try it. Can't I try it for awhile even?"

Grandma's beady little eyes were even beadier than usual, watching me close.

"You've got a screw loose if you think I'm going to make special meals just for you," said Beth.

Beth had used up any good feelings I had left over from yesterday. "I'll make my own meals. Promise."

"It'll take us all summer to eat what we have already." Dad nodded at the piles of food on the counter that church members and neighbors and relatives had brought over in the last two days – *platz*, cookies, cakes, buns. There were casseroles, *hollopchee*, *varenika*, and at least three pies in the freezer. It was enough to make me wonder if there was maybe a commandment I didn't know about that said you had to bring food to your neighbors when someone was sick. Only problem was that most of it had meat in it. Or else it was bread.

I was desperate. "If Mom was here she'd buy me this stuff," I muttered just loud enough to be heard.

Grandma shook her head. Dad stared at me over top of his paper. He stared for a long time. "Do what you want," he finally said.

"Thanks, Dad!" I gave him a bear hug, carefully avoiding his whiskers.

"Unbelievable," Beth muttered.

She was such a sore loser, even though I knew using Mom like that was sort of dirty pool. Only I didn't have a whole lot of options. I poured a glass of milk and piled my plate with cheese, carrot sticks, and fruit. Grandma got up to cut the chocolate cake for dessert. I asked for an extra big piece.

"I thought you were giving up bread," said Beth.

"This is cake."

"Cake is bread, *dummkopp*."

She must've been too ticked to even think of a good insult. "It is?" I looked at Dad.

All he did was shrug. "Leave me out of this."

Beth couldn't wait to gloat. "Any grain or anything made with grain or flour counts as a bread." She started counting things off on her fingers. "Cookies, muffins, cake, pie, donuts, pancakes, rice, macaroni –"

"Macaroni?!" Who knew? She had to be pulling a fast one on me.

"*Nah, meyahl?*" said Grandma quietly. "Lying has short legs, not? It doesn't get you very far. By now you should've learned yourself that much."

"I never lied." Maybe I hadn't told the whole truth, but I'd never lied. Not today anyways.

Beth grabbed my list and crossed off at least half the stuff on it. "Still think you're going to give up bread and meat?"

I thought about throwing my glass of milk in her smug ugly face. "I hate you," I muttered and stomped out the door to eat in the sunshine.

So much for getting along with Beth. I could practically feel God frowning at me.

Outside Tommy rubbed up against my arm, nosing at my plate. "This is going to be a lot harder than I thought, Tom-cat."

Tommy didn't give a care about my troubles. He sat on his haunches beside his empty saucer. "*Meow,*" he accused me. Rats. I'd forgotten to feed him. Again. I dumped half my milk in his saucer and chewed on a carrot stick.

Lena followed me out to the porch with a huge piece of chocolate cake. "Dad says we can go swimming again tomorrow. My sunburn is almost better." She shoved a forkful of cake in her mouth.

"Mmmmm." She smacked her lips. "*Schmack gout.*"

Why couldn't I have been an only child?

I didn't even feel bad later when Beth went out for groceries and I used her razor to practice shaving my legs. It was going pretty good, too, and then Lena started banging on the bathroom door, which you bet I'd remembered to lock.

"I'm in here!" I yelled.

"Hurry up! I have to go!"

"Just get lost for once! I'm busy."

"I have to go nowww! Pleeaase! Let me in!"

She kept banging and yelling and the more she banged and yelled, the faster I went and the madder I got. Before I knew it I'd sliced a nice big chunk off my shin. The blood started to pour out of the slice and Holy Moses, it stung like crazy when I washed it off, enough to bring tears to my eyes.

By now Lena was crying outside the door and I would've let her in already, except my leg was still gushing.

I let Lena in as soon as I could. "All right already. I'm finished."

Her face was a blotchy mess. "I couldn't wait," she mumbled.

Fuy. So it goes. "Why do you always have to wait until you can't hold it?"

She just stood there, wiping her runny nose with the back of her hand.

"Never mind. Take off those shorts already."

While she cleaned herself up and changed clothes I rinsed out the wet ones and washed the floor. Lena went back outside to play and I went back to scrubbing the garage siding with one shaved leg and one hairy leg because there wasn't enough time to finish the job before Beth got home.

❧

Dear God,

I don't really hate Beth. Only sometimes I feel like I do. She just makes me so mad.

You knew what I meant when I said I wouldn't eat any bread, didn't you? You knew I only meant bread *bread, and not all that other stuff, right? I'll try my best to give up most bread, but I think I'll starve to death if I can't eat rice or macaroni or cereal even.*

Thanks for making Lena's sunburn better. I couldn't stand having to spend another whole day around here when all my friends are at the pool – even though I got a lot of work done on the garage. So far I've made nine dollars already!

Please help Beth to not be such a grouch, and help Lena to not bug me so much. I'm sorry about Lena's accident, I didn't mean to be mean to her. And I know it's wrong to use Beth's stuff without asking, which is probably what you were trying to tell me when I cut myself. That was like, some kind of karma, right?

Most of all, please take care of Mom and help her to get well soon. Lena and I miss her. I guess Beth and Dad do, too. Maybe that's why everyone's so crabby all the time.

Amen.

9

She sits herself on her ears

"You weren't kidding!" Jillian cruised into the backyard on her bike.

"Hey!" I set down the wire brush I'd been using and grabbing a corner of the scaffold, I jumped to the ground. The frame rocked and rattled back in place.

"Careful, *kint*," Grandma warned. She and Auntie Nettie sat on lawn chairs in the shade, shelling ice-cream pails of peas as fast as Lena and Beth picked them.

"I had to see this for myself," grinned Jillian.

"Check out the tan." I pulled aside the strap on my bikini top to show her how tanned I was already in only three days on the job.

Grandma clucked her tongue. "*Schentlich*," she muttered, followed by a stream of Plautdietsch that made Auntie Nettie chuckle.

"What's so funny?" Sometimes it really got my goat when they talked about me in Low German.

"Grandma says you sit yourself on your ears," said Auntie Nettie, grinning still more. "She means you don't listen."

Jillian cracked up. "I can totally see it."

"My grandma doesn't approve," I whispered, rolling my eyes. "She and Beth think Dad's crazy to let me paint, and that I'm plain wicked to be parading around half-naked."

"Your friend would like something cold to drink maybe?" Auntie Nettie asked.

I offered to get lemonade for everyone. Even went around to the garden to ask Beth and Lena if they wanted a break.

Beth took one look at me and said, "Put on some clothes at least."

There was no point in trying to be nice to her. I was perfectly respectable in a pair of old cut-offs and my bikini top. "What's wrong now?"

"For one thing, you look ridiculous wearing a top like that. It's not like you have anything to show off."

My face grew hot. "Thanks for noticing."

Beth could go jump in a lake as far as I was concerned, but I pulled on a T-shirt anyways. Partly for the sake of peace, and partly because I wondered if Beth might be a little bit right about me looking ridiculous.

When I came out with the lemonade, Grandma had put Jillian to work already, shelling peas. I should've known Grandma couldn't stand to see idle hands.

"So? How goes the big job?" Auntie Nettie squinted at the house.

Personally, I don't know what Tom Sawyer made all the fuss about. I knew this was only my third day at it, but so far I liked this painting thing. It was fun hosing off the loose dirt. I liked scraping and brushing blistered paint from the window frames and siding. I liked smoothing the rough edges with sandpaper.

I liked how Tommy stretched out on the porch to keep me company, snoozing in the sun or just watching and listening to the radio and me jabbering away at him. I liked how the sun warmed my bare back as I worked. And for sure I liked being out of earshot of Beth all morning.

Most of all, I liked how Dad nodded after work when he checked how much I'd done and said, "Good job." He'd even asked me to do the bottom half of the house. I could've done the top part, too, but he wouldn't let me climb so high on the scaffolding.

We still hadn't got around to the actual painting part, but I was pretty sure I was going to like that, too. Maybe Grandma was on to something with this work thing.

"The garage is ready," I said. "And one side of the house. Dad's going to caulk windows this weekend. He thinks we'll be painting by next week, as long as it doesn't rain."

Grandma shook her head. "*Uy uy uy.*"

"Enough already, *mumke*," tutted Auntie Nettie. "It never bothers anyone and she's doing a real good job."

"I'm doing a real good job of picking peas, right Auntie Nettie?" Lena asked. "Mom will be surprised, right?"

"Best job ever," nodded Auntie Nettie. "Your mother will be proud of you. This afternoon we'll blanch and freeze them yet, too."

Lena beamed.

Beth picked up her pail. "C'mon, *schnigglefritz*. One more row to go yet."

"I've got to get home, but I'll see you at the pool this afternoon, right?" Jillian handed me her empty glass.

"For sure."

"Uh, say hi to your Mom for me."

"I will." I wasn't sure exactly if she knew Mom was sick, but I wasn't about to talk about it right then.

I gathered the rest of the empty glasses. Auntie Nettie followed me inside with a brimming bowl of peas. "*Nah, meyahl?* You didn't tell your friend your mother was sick?"

"I will. Just not, you know, in front of everybody. She probably knows anyways."

"But not from you." She dumped the peas into the big colander in the sink and started rinsing. "Only from the *schnetke* conference."

She'd lost me. "The what?"

"The biscuit conference. You know, the gossips."

Auntie Nettie made it sound like I was ashamed of my mother or something. That wasn't it at all. Mom just wasn't a subject that came up in casual conversation.

"Esther will be home again in no time," Auntie Nettie smiled at me. "You'll see. Are you remembering to say your prayers for her?"

"Yeah." That's all everyone said – pray, pray, pray. I *was* praying. Every night.

"Have you been yet to see her?"

"We haven't been allowed. Maybe tomorrow, Dad says." Part of me was a little bit glad we hadn't been able to go see Mom yet.

"*Ach!*" Auntie Nettie shook her head. "What nonsense is that? Esther will worry herself crazy. And children need their mother."

I smiled, but Auntie Nettie didn't seem to notice. "Anyways, Dad says she mostly sleeps right now," I prompted, hoping she might let slip something I should know.

"Sure she sleeps, who wouldn't sleep when –" Auntie Nettie turned the cold water on full blast, mumbling to herself. "They are fools, those doctors. They think they are like God and know everything that is best for your mother. What have they done for her all these years? I'll tell you. *Nusht.* Worse than *nusht.*"

I'd always known my mother was different. Nobody else's mother did stuff like cry over dead baby robins. Or put on their bathing suits to go outside and play with their kids in the rain during a thunderstorm. Or pick dandelions and weeds to put in a vase on the kitchen table.

When I was little and Beth was in school already, Mom used to take me for long walks all over town. One time in the spring we took off our socks and shoes. I rolled up my pants and Mom tied up her skirt above her knees and we spent the whole afternoon splashing and wading in the ditches looking for tadpoles. I'd never had so much fun. Only when Dad came home that night for supper he said his boss at work had seen Mom and me playing in the ditches and asked him if his wife was "*gaunz ferekt*," which meant totally crazy.

"So? What did you tell him?" she wanted to know.

Dad smiled kind of crooked and shook his head and said, "Not totally crazy, only halfway."

Which made Mom laugh. Then Dad put his arms around her waist and kissed her laughing mouth and Mom twirled me up in her arms and said, "Elsie and I went on an adventure this afternoon, didn't we *schnigglefritz*?"

After that, whenever Mom got one of her crazy ideas – like maybe climbing a tree to see if there were eggs inside a nest – then she always said, "Do you feel like an adventure, *schnigglefritz*?"

Only pretty soon after that Lena was born, so she became the *schnigglefritz* in our house. And then I started school yet, and found out other kids didn't go on adventures with their mothers. They mostly only played on the playground at the park.

Auntie Nettie shook her head, still muttering mostly to herself. "It's not my business. I shouldn't go so much off at the mouth."

I grinned. We all knew Auntie Nettie's opinion of psychiatrists. We all knew Auntie Nettie's opinions about most things. "You're probably right. I bet her doctor is a real *dummkopp*," I teased.

"*En schozzle. En daugnichts.*" Auntie Nettie chuckled. She flicked her wet hands, spritzing me with water. "Good thing you don't know the Plautdietsch."

"I know some."

Dad walked in about then, home for lunch. "What do you know, Elsie?"

Auntie Nettie got busy at the sink real quick, her back turned. But her shoulders shook silently. I broke up laughing.

"Why do I think you two have been up to no good?" Dad hung up his cap.

"Sit you *doy*, O'Lloyd," Auntie Nettie ordered him into a chair. For sure there was no one named O'Lloyd in our family. But once, Grandma Redekop said that to a visitor named O'Lloyd when she didn't know the right English way to say "Sit over there." Now everyone said it all the time.

Dad didn't bother to protest. Not that Auntie Nettie would've listened. She winked at me. "*Putzendonna*," she whispered. "You'll get me in trouble."

"Better you than me," I whispered back. Then because it felt so good to laugh I threw my arms around her waist and hugged her.

"*Uy uy uy*," she said, patting my hair.

For lunch Auntie Nettie had brought over two bagfuls of *rollkuchen* to eat with watermelon. She knew it was my favorite food in the world. I'd poured a lake of syrup into my plate beside a mountain of the deep-fried dough strips before I saw Beth smirking at me and realized that *roll-kuchen* was probably bread, too. *Fuy*.

Sighing, I gave my plate to Lena. "I think I'll just have watermelon and yogurt."

Everyone stopped doing whatever it was they were doing. They turned, like they were all tied to the same string, to stare at me.

"Are you sick?" Dad asked.

Grandma felt my forehead, "You don't feel hot. You should lie down maybe."

I started laughing again. Pretty soon I was laughing so hard my stomach hurt. I couldn't stop till I got the hiccups.

Dear God, I prayed that night. My stomach grumbled.

It was kind of mean of Beth to say I don't fill out my bathing suit enough for anyone to notice. Not that I give a care really, even if it's true. I don't want Aaron to notice me for that, I just want him to notice me. At the pool today it was like he didn't know I was alive even.

I know it's only been three days so far, but I need to change our deal a little. Instead of giving up meat and bread, would it be okay if I just gave up meat? I don't think I'll make it twenty-one days otherwise. For sure not in this house. Daniel wasn't a Mennonite.

Thanks for understanding, God.

Most of all, please let it be your will for my mother to get well again soon. Dad says we can go see her tomorrow. Only I'm not sure I want to yet.

In Jesus' name, Amen.

❧

My stomach was growling so much I couldn't sleep, so I slipped downstairs and helped myself to a huge plate of *rollkuchen* drowned in syrup.

10

Only good

"Lookit once how high I can go, Elsie."

Lena, that little monkey, dangled hand over hand from the scaffolding. A minute ago she'd been drawing chalk pictures on the sidewalk.

"Get off of there!"

"Aren't you done yet? Let's go see Mom."

"Almost."

"That's what you said before, like an hour ago. Can I help?"

"I told you already, you're too little still." I leaned on the wire brush as I scrubbed the top corners of the bay window one more time. Really though, I was dawdling, putting off going to Eden a few minutes longer. Suddenly the scaffold shuddered, catching me off balance. I grabbed a support to steady myself then looked to see what the problem was. Lena was spread-eagled across the crossbar and reaching still higher.

"Lena Margaret Redekop, get down this instant!"

She ignored me. "I'm climbing Dad's jungle gym."

"It's not a jungle gym, it's a scaffold. And it's not for playing on. You know that." By then Lena had climbed all the way up beside me. Tommy leaped down as she scrambled across the boards.

"*Fuy*," she scoffed. "I could jump to the ground from here. Bet I could climb as high as Dad even." She tilted her head back, checking out the top level of the scaffolding.

"Don't even think it." I scrambled over the edge, then held my hand out to Lena. "C'mon. I'll help you down."

She scooted over to the other side, swung off the platform and jumped down by herself. Then she grinned at me, all cheek. "Now can we go see Mom?"

"Not until you promise to stay off the scaffolding. Dad'll kill me if I let anything happen to you."

She stuck her tongue out at me. "Promise."

Beth wouldn't let us out of the house, though, until we ate lunch and looked "presentable." Shorts and T-shirts weren't good enough for her. "You can't go to visit Mom looking like a couple of rug rats. She'll think the whole house is falling apart."

"What's wrong now?" I asked.

"Look at your feet – they're filthy. And Lena's are worse. Don't either of you ever wear shoes?"

Okay, so maybe she had a point. "All right already. We'll wash our feet. C'mon, Lena."

"And put on a blouse and sandals," she called after us. "And brush your hair!"

She had to give us a final inspection yet before she let us out the front door. "What happened to your leg?"

The razor slice on my leg had been healing pretty well till I'd scratched the scab off this morning. I said the first thing that came to me. "I banged my shin on my bike pedal."

"Well don't pick at it. You'll get a scar. Are you sure you don't want me to drive you?"

Beth was such an old woman. It wasn't like we'd never been to Eden before. Besides which, it was only ten minutes away by bike, and then we could head straight to the pool after.

From the outside, Eden looked more like an old folks' home than a hospital. We dropped our bikes on the front lawn. My heart was pounding already as we walked through the two sets of double glass doors leading to the lobby.

"*Fuy*," Lena wrinkled her nose. "It stinks."

"Shhh," I hushed her. For sure she was right about the smell, though. No amount of Pine-Sol could cover it up. The place smelled of sick people, all shut in together. It made me wonder if maybe that was how sadness and heartache and hopelessness smelled, and how anyone could get well in a place like this. And then right away I was thinking of the other times I'd visited Mom here, even after I thought I'd forgotten them.

All of a sudden I was angry. Why should a smell make me angry?

"Elsie?" Lena tugged on my blouse.

My feet dragged me to the front desk. "Can you tell us where Esther Redekop is?" I wished my voice didn't sound so little. "Please."

"I think I saw her in the lounge," the nurse nodded. "Right through there."

We knew the way.

Lena and I walked through another set of doors into the lounge. I scanned the groups of stiff couches and chairs and checked the line of tables along the windows that looked into the courtyard. Sometimes we played *knippsbrat* with Mom there, or else shuffleboard at the long table at the other end of the room. A group of patients sat in front of a TV in one corner. In another corner stood a piano, all closed up. A few more patients sat by themselves, holding a book or magazine, but mostly they weren't reading. Mostly they were just staring into space.

Holy Moses. I glanced at one blank face after another, looking away again quickly before all those empty eyes could pull me in. I'm telling you I was relieved something fierce to find Mom wasn't among them. They reminded me of zombies, or maybe robots. They only seemed human until you looked into their eyes. Then you knew. Then you could see they were mostly dead inside.

I'd almost forgot how much I hated this place. My mother didn't belong here.

I pulled my shoulders back and made believe my mission was to guide Lena past all the nurses, doctors, and zombie patients to rescue our mother.

"Where is she?" Lena whispered, slipping her hand into mine.

If I went back to the desk to ask again, I might leave altogether. "Maybe she has the same room as before. C'mon."

A hallway opened off the other side of the lounge. Walking along the corridor, we peeked in open doors and checked nameplates and pretty soon we found her.

"Mom!" Lena practically shouted.

Mom looked up from the book she was reading. She smiled to see us there. The smile didn't reach her eyes or light up her face like a smile is supposed to, but she did smile anyways.

I hung back a little, but Lena right away threw her arms around Mom and hugged with all her might.

Mom laughed softly. "Oh, my. This is quite the greeting. Surely I haven't been away so long already for you to miss me so much?"

Lena spread her arms out wide. "I've missed you this much!"

"I've missed you this much, too, *schnigglefritz*. I've missed you to the moon and back again." She scooped Lena up in her arms and hugged her tight, smiling at me over Lena's shoulder, until Lena finally squirmed free.

My heart was thudding in my chest still. Mom didn't act like she was mad at me. I quickly kissed her forehead and tried not to let it show on my face that she smelled funny. Or that she looked so awfully tired. Her eyes didn't shine like they usually did. Mom was maybe starting to turn into one of the zombies.

"Let's go for a walk," I blurted, because I had to get out of there and I had to get Mom out of there, too. "Are you thirsty? I'm thirsty. Let's go get a soft drink."

Mom moved slowly. I almost had to drag her, back out through the lounge and past the reception desk. She told the nurse she'd be outside with her daughters.

Outside Mom's eyes didn't look so dead anymore. We walked across the street to the service station. Mom didn't have any money on her, but I had brought some change. I dropped fifteen cents into the slot and slid a bottle of Grape Crush out of the rack for Lena. Mom wanted an Orange Crush, and I got myself a Mountain Dew.

Then we walked back to Eden with our soft drinks and sat on a bench on the back lawn.

"So, how goes it?" I didn't know what else to say, and I wanted for Mom to say, "On two legs, like a gander," because then we could smile and maybe even pretend everything was like always.

Only Mom had gone somewheres, just for a second. Then she said, "*Blous gout*," and chuckled at the puzzled looks we gave her. "It means, only good, just good. Your grandfather used to say it all the time."

"Were you thinking about him or something?"

"I guess I was. Never mind about me. How're you girls doing? Tell me how things are at home."

"*Blous gout*," I said. At least it got a little smile out of Mom. And it was true, sort of. Things weren't going great, but I guess they could've been going worse yet.

"Are you girls getting along?"

"Sure. Mostly." What was I supposed to say? It wasn't like I could tell her that Beth was a bossy old bag or that Lena was pestering me all the time or that Dad was already pulling his hair out. We weren't supposed to get her worked up worrying herself over us.

"Is someone remembering to feed Tommy?"

I nodded. "Sure. I'm taking care of him." I'd have to remember to fill his saucer when I got home. I was pretty sure I'd forgotten that morning.

After that I didn't know what else to say. Good thing Lena was with. She gabbed away about how Beth was in charge and how she was helping take care of the house. How she'd gotten sunburned and I was painting the house and had decided to be a "veternarian," but Beth thought it was stupid. How we were remembering to say our prayers every night.

Mom didn't even pick up on the veternarian thing. I didn't bother to correct Lena. I could see from Mom's eyes that she wasn't really listening anyways.

"*Nah yo*, it sounds like you're doing just fine without me." It was Mom's voice talking, but it wasn't Mom. This person was a robot filling in for her while the real Mom was far away somewheres.

Just fine? Hadn't she heard a thing Lena said?

"I swam across the pool three times last week," Lena was talking a mile a minute still. "Pretty soon I'll be able to go in the deep end."

"Won't that be wonderful?" said the robot Mom. "I'd like to see that."

"You can. Come swimming with us." Lena tugged on her arm, trying to get her to stand up.

Mom smiled. "Oh, not today, *schnigglefritz*. I can't today."

"Yes you can. Just stand up and come with."

Something flashed across Mom's face. Just like that she looked small, smaller than Lena even. She just sort of crumpled. She shook her head and pulled away.

Lena's lower lip trembled like it did when she was getting ready to bawl her eyes out. Before she could get going I stood up and put my hand on her shoulder, squeezing a little bit so maybe she'd get it that she shouldn't cry. "Mom can watch you swim another day. You still have to get all practiced up anyways."

She nodded, whispering. "Don't worry, Mom. You can watch me swim another day."

"That sounds good." Mom gave Lena a weak smile.

A few minutes later we walked Robot Mom to her room and kissed her good-bye. "We'll come back soon," I promised.

"I think I'll put my ear a bit on the mattress," she said, sitting down on the bed and still trying to smile at us.

"Do you want me to put out the light?"

Mom nodded. "Take care of each other," she said. "I love you, girls."

"We love you, too, Mom," I whispered.

"Get better soon." Lena stuck her head back through the door for one last wave.

And then we were hurrying down the corridor, through the lounge, and bursting out the front door, running for our bikes.

"Mom doesn't look sick," Lena said. "How come she has to stay in there?"

"She's not sick on the outside. She's sick on the inside." I grabbed my bike.

"Because of your pajama party," Lena said, out of the blue.

My blood turned cold. "I'll race you," I said. "You can have a head start."

I pedaled just hard enough to stay behind her, even rode part way with no hands.

Far enough to wish I didn't ever have to visit Mom in that place ever again. I wished it twice. I didn't give a care that conditions didn't favor my wish coming true.

Dear God,

How come I feel worse after seeing Mom? I didn't even have any fun at the pool after. Sadie and Jillian and Aaron and Pete and everyone were telling jokes and goofing off like always, but I didn't feel one bit like laughing. Anyways, nothing they said was funny. It was all stupid and childish.

I know they're supposed to be helping Mom and everything, but I hate that place. Mom's no crazier than other people, so I don't know why she should even be in there. If she's crazy, then probably I am, too. Maybe they should lock me up, too.

Sometimes I think Auntie Nettie is right. Sometimes I think those doctors don't have a clue how to help Mom. It's like they're making her worse instead of better.

I don't understand how it could be your will for Mom to be in that place. It's not fair for her to have to go there just because I was bad. Please, please, God, help her get better soon. Really better. Not just well enough to come home, but well enough so she never has to go back there. Not ever.

Amen.

11

Biscuit conference

Mark Giesbrecht is a first-class, good-for-nothing dork.

I was lying there at the pool minding my own business, soaking up the sun. He sits himself down and starts eating *knackzote*, which is no problem until he starts spitting the shells down my bathing suit top. He didn't do it to anyone else, just me. I had to go into the change room to get them all out.

"If you ask me, I think he likes you," said Jillian.

We'd taken over her backyard for our first pajama party of the summer.

"That's an understatement," Heather mumbled, her face buried in her arms. "He's always picking on you." I was sitting on her bum, kneading her back and shoulders.

"Ow!" she squirmed. "What's with you? Take it easy already."

"Sorry." Beside me, Sadie was giving Naomi a back rub and beside them, Joy was giving Jillian a back rub. It was Eleanor's turn to sit out. "He bugs me. I wish he'd just leave me alone for once."

"Give the guy a break," said Sadie. "Mark's not so bad."

Sadie, defending Mark? She'd been acting a little weird the last couple of days, but sticking up for Mark wasn't a little weird. It was – bizarre.

"Mark's okay, I guess," Joy said, grinning. "But he's no Pete Wiens, eh Jillian?"

Sadie snorted.

"'Fess up, Jill." Eleanor got right in Jillian's face. "Has he or hasn't he?"

"Has he or hasn't he what?"

"Kissed you, you fool!"

"Time," Jillian announced. She ignored the question purely for the pleasure of tormenting us. "Pete and I just like to hang out. We're buddies."

"If you say so," said Sadie. Grinning, she reached over to crank up the radio. Donny Osmond was singing "Puppy Love," and she started crooning along with him.

Jillian thwacked Sadie with a pillow, but she was out-numbered. We all howled out the words to the song, laughing ourselves silly and dodging Jillian's pillow as we switched places.

In ten minutes we'd switch again and so on, until everyone gave six back rubs and got six back rubs. It was a pajama party ritual, whether we slept inside or out, like

tonight. We'd put our sleeping bags in a circle around a
pile of junk food and Jillian's transistor radio.

"You might as well tell us," Joy coaxed. "We'll weasel
it out of you sooner or later."

"Hah! See my halo?"

Heather, sitting on Jillian's bum, lifted two chunks of
her hair. "More like devil horns."

Right away Naomi gasped. "Don't say such a thing!"

"Holy flippin' Moses," Heather rolled her eyes.

"Hey you guys. Lets not fight over it." Eleanor, the
peacemaker, nipped the argument in the bud.

Usually we were pretty careful to avoid subjects that
upset Naomi, which included pretty much anything
about the devil or witches or magic. Her parents were
awfully religious, even for Hopefield. They were even
more strict than Eleanor's parents, and Eleanor's parents
had been missionaries in South America and everything.

"Anyway, Pete's far too shy to do anything except ride
home with me," grinned Jillian.

"Maybe you could get him to ride home with you
along *schmungestrasse*," said Eleanor, adding a long drawn
out kissing sound.

The rest of us were too astonished to speak. We were
for sure all thinking the same thing – what the heck did
Eleanor know about lover's lane?

Eleanor giggled nervously. "I just heard stuff, you
know, from my older sister."

Jillian bailed her out. "I'll probably just wait for a Sadie Hawkins Dance so I can ask him out."

"Fat chance," said Heather.

"Why?" Jillian looked up at the sudden silence. "What?"

"You poor misguided child." Sadie put a hand over her heart and used her best preacher's voice.

No one knew how to tell Jillian that she had about as much chance of going to a Sadie Hawkins Dance in Hopefield as she had of flying to the moon. Then I remembered the old joke Beth used to say all the time before she was saved.

"I could've danced all night," I sang. "But I'm a Mennonite."

"What's that supposed to mean?" Jillian demanded.

"This is Hopefield, remember?"

"So?"

"We don't dance. Dancing is a sin. Right up there with smoking, drinking, playing cards, going to movies, and just about anything else that's fun. Haven't you noticed we don't have a movie theater in this town even?" Seven churches, but no movie theater.

For just a minute, I tried to imagine how it would be to dance with Aaron Penner. His hand on my waist, my hand on his shoulder, smiling up into his gorgeous blue eyes. It might happen. Maybe. Like if someone we both knew got married and there was a social after the wedding, and we were both invited.

As if. The others were already gossiping about someone Sadie had seen parked on lover's lane. The biscuit conference was going pretty good all right.

The sun had set a while ago, and the first stars twinkled faintly. We hardly needed sleeping bags even, the night was so warm.

                      ✒

We waited until it was completely dark, the entire town sleeping already, before we crept out the back gate.

"That was too easy," said Joy.

"Shhh!!!"

Laughing, wide awake, and breathless, we ran down the alley.

"Where are we going?" Heather asked.

"It's a surprise," said Jillian. "Follow me."

"Not another one of Jillian's surprises," groaned Eleanor. She traipsed along behind us, but she wasn't all that happy about it.

Jillian led us down the route we'd planned, sticking to back alleys as much as possible. By the time we reached the park, we were all pretty wound up and acting like little kids. We ran for the slides and swings, whooping and hollering at half volume.

"Over here!" I called. Everyone grabbed a spot on the wobbly old merry-go-round. We ran, pushing it faster and faster and still faster, then hopping on one by one. I was the last to jump on and lean out, breathless, letting the night sky spin dizzily around and around and around some more.

"That was so neat," Joy finally sighed, when the merry-go-round stopped.

"It gets better," said Jillian. "C'mon."

We chased each other through the park to the big elm tree close by the fence that surrounded the pool. Deck lights shimmered on the quiet water.

A shadow moved in the bushes. "You're late."

Heather strangled a scream.

Aaron stepped into the light. "We thought you weren't going to show up." Behind him Mark, Pete, and the other guys rustled their way out of hiding.

The midnight rendezvous had been the boys' idea. They'd dared Jillian, Sadie, and me that afternoon, when they heard about Jillian's party. We just hadn't told anyone else. The others would never have followed us if they'd known what we planned.

"Let's go." Mark headed toward the pool.

Naomi looked around nervously. "We really shouldn't be here, should we? Isn't there a NO TRESPASSING sign somewheres?"

Jillian held up her pack. "I brought our bathing suits. We're not the first ones to ever go for a midnight swim."

Joy teetered like she might faint.

It wasn't like we were planning on wrecking anything. We weren't delinquents. And we were all real good swimmers. Besides which, the guys were climbing the chain-link fence already.

"I don't know," Eleanor whispered. "We'll be in big trouble if we're caught. I'm pretty sure there's a fine, you know –"

"Stay here then." Jillian began climbing. "It's your funeral."

In the end, everyone except Naomi and Joy went over the fence. To be honest, I was more than a little nervous, too, but no way was I going to be left out. Especially after I ruined everything for everyone last week already. Jillian and Sadie would really think I was a wimp.

At first I was looking over my shoulder too much to have any fun. But then after a while, when no alarms went off or anything, I started to enjoy myself. I lay on my back at the bottom of the pool, staring up at the silhouetted bodies moving above me. Light streamed around them.

Everything seemed unreal, as if the night had put a spell over us. Only I felt more real and alive than I could ever remember. I felt bigger than life. I wanted to hug Jillian. I'd never think of doing something like this without her.

I didn't want the spell to end. Only I couldn't hold my breath much longer. I let myself rise slowly, quietly breaking the surface.

"This is the best."

The voice behind me was barely a whisper, and a little husky, but I'd know Aaron's voice anywhere. Treading water, I turned, smiling, all ready to agree with him. The night, the moment, everything was perfect.

Only thing was, Aaron wasn't talking to me. He didn't even know I was there. He was talking to Sadie. Which wasn't a big deal, except the way his voice sounded I knew he wasn't just talking to her, he was talking *only* to her. And he didn't just mean that swimming at night was the best, he meant swimming at night *with her* was the best.

I dove deep and swam toward the others. Sadie and Aaron were right behind me. Probably, it meant nothing I told myself. Nothing at all. Absolutely *nusht*.

But for sure I didn't believe me.

We formed a circle in the deep end, treading water and talking. I didn't say much because my head was too full of questions. Why hadn't I noticed something going on before? It must have all started while I was grounded. That figured. That's why Sadie had been acting weird.

"Someone's coming!" Naomi hissed from the other side of the fence. A car slowed as it drove by on the street. A patrol car. "It's the police!"

Naomi and Joy disappeared. The rest of us didn't have time to get out of the pool. We ducked underwater, surfacing against the side of the pool under the diving boards and keeping our heads below the deck. Almost right away, before the water stopped rippling even, a patrol car swung up to the fence. Headlights scanned the pool. Holy Moses.

"C'mon out!"

A disembodied voice from some kind of loudspeaker crackled over our heads. It reached right into my stomach. I thought I might lose it right then and there.

"What do we do?" groaned Heather.

"Shhh!" Jillian put a finger to her lips. "Don't move."

"We know you're in there," the voice crackled again. "You might as well come out."

"We better give ourselves up," whispered Eleanor.

"Are you totally nuts?" Aaron hissed.

We huddled still closer, staying low. Mark was pressed against me on one side, Jillian on the other. Mark and I were staring into each other's bright eyes. I was pretty sure I could feel his heart racing as fast as mine.

I don't know how long we huddled there. Probably only a few minutes, even though it felt like forever. Our teeth were chattering before we finally heard the car drive away.

"Wait," Mark said. "Just a bit longer yet."

The patrol car appeared on the street. It drove by slowly, then turned the corner away from the park.

"Now!" Pete boosted himself out of the water. We bolted, grabbing our clothes and racing for the fence.

"That was wild," said Mark.

I nodded, getting all tangled up as I tried to pull my T-shirt on over my wet bathing suit. "It'll get wilder yet if we're caught." *Please God*, I prayed, *help us get out of here without getting caught and I swear I'll never do anything like this again.*

I wasn't the only one praying, that was for sure.

"Never again. Never again." Heather's teeth chattered, her voice shook as she scrambled up the fence. "I promise I'll never ever break the law again."

Jimmy, Pete, and Caleb were the first ones to hurdle over the fence. They dropped to the ground on the other side. Jillian and Heather were right behind. Right about then is when the cop car pulled up in the alley across the street, facing the pool. For a split second everyone froze.

Aaron, Mark, and Sadie were straddling the top of the fence still. Eleanor and I were clinging halfway up. Then Aaron hit the ground running.

"Meet you at home!" Jillian took off with the others.

Mark reached down and grabbed my hand. He hauled me up and over. "Jump!"

I practically flew I jumped so far. The landing took my breath away. The cops had turned onto the street and were speeding toward the parking entrance.

"I'm caught!" Sadie cried. Her suit was snagged on the fence. She yanked at it, tottering back and forth. Eleanor had pretty much given up, falling back to the ground. Her hands clasped the chain links from the other side. She stared, wild-eyed at me. Aaron brushed past on his way back to help.

I'd lost sight of the cop car behind the building. For a second I thought about going back to help, too. Then I heard tires squealing. I stopped thinking and started running. I ducked through the trees, dove under the hedge bordering the park, and elbowed my way out the other side into the fair grounds. Scrambling to my feet I ran, flat out, right into a barbed wire fence, flipped head over heels yet, rolled, and was up again, still running.

At some point I realized I was running beside someone. I didn't know it was Heather until we both cut through a garden and into Jillian's backyard. We almost knocked over Jillian, Naomi, and Joy.

"Never again," croaked Heather, gasping for breath. She fell onto the lawn. "My heart can't take anymore."

"Where's Sadie? And Eleanor?" asked Jillian.

I shook my head. Leaning forward, hands on my knees, I tried to catch my breath. "What do we do now?"

We did the only thing we could do. We waited. And waited. And waited some more yet.

We were about ready to wake up Jillian's parents, never mind the consequences, when Sadie and Eleanor stumbled in the back gate and fell onto the lawn. Eleanor burst into tears as we crowded around.

"What happened?" asked Jillian. "We thought you were right behind us."

Sadie waited to catch her breath. "Elsie knew I was caught on the fence."

The night was too dark to see very well, but I could feel her eyes blazing right through me. "I thought Aaron went to help you."

"He did. He was really great. He got me loose while Mark helped Eleanor. She was petrified." She scowled, disgusted, at Eleanor. "Mark jumped down and shoved her under those spruce trees, you know, the ones in the corner."

We nodded, holding our breath practically through Sadie's whole story. How it was too late by then for Mark to get out again or find another place to hide. How Aaron and Sadie, watching from the bushes, saw the police take him away. Then Aaron and Sadie went back for Eleanor, but it took them forever to convince her to leave her hiding place.

"Aaron had to climb back over the fence and practically drag her out," said Sadie.

"I couldn't help it," Eleanor sniffed. "I was too scared to move."

"We looked for you," Sadie said to me. "But you'd disappeared."

There wasn't much I could say. "I-I panicked," I stammered. "All I could think about was getting out of there. It didn't matter anyways. I couldn't have done anything more to help."

Only it did matter. Sadie knew it. I knew it. And for sure everyone else knew it.

"Anyways," Sadie turned to the others. "Aaron walked us back here. He's going to call Mark in the morning and then let us know what happened."

Yeah, I thought. *I bet that was a real hardship. Walking all the way back in the dark with Aaron.* I hated myself for thinking what I was thinking. But I couldn't help it.

No one could sleep. We lay awake for hours, whispering and retelling the story. Running away from the police yet. How stupid could we get? Eventually we couldn't help but laugh at ourselves over it.

I laughed with the others on the outside, but on the inside I wasn't laughing. None of the heroes in any book I'd ever read would have abandoned their friends like I did. I was despicable; a coward who only thought of saving her own skin. It was a miserable thing to find out about yourself.

In my heart of hearts, I wondered if I might have gone back, even if I hadn't seen Aaron and Sadie together in the pool. I suspected I was not only a coward, but a jealous, spiteful coward to boot.

Jillian and Sadie were whispering, heads close, too quietly for me to hear. I turned away.

Who'd have thought that Mark Giesbrecht, of all people, would turn out to be a hero?

❧

Dear God –

I'm such a loser. I left Sadie caught on the fence because I was jealous, and now she hates me. This should have been the best night of my life. Instead I feel lousy.

Why does Aaron have to like Sadie and not me? It's not fair, God. I can't say sorry to Sadie. I just can't. Not yet.

Please forgive all my trespasses. There's too many to tell you about, but I guess you know what they are. And watch over Mom. This would never have happened if Mom had been home. I'd never have gotten grounded and then Sadie and Aaron . . . I need Mom to come home again.

Are you listening, God? It doesn't feel like you're listening.

Amen.

12

She stirred her own mouse

Mark didn't tell the police who all was with him. But we got together first thing in the morning and decided it wasn't right for him to take all the blame. So we rode over to the police station on our bikes and turned ourselves in.

The officer at the desk took down our names.

When I told him mine he said, "You're Isaak Redekop's daughter, aren't you?"

Holy Moses. I nodded miserably. I could already hear Dad saying how I'd stirred my own *mouse* and now I was going to have to eat it yet, too. And that wouldn't be the half of it. Maybe I'd get out of my room by Christmas. I knew I was going to have to come clean before he heard about our midnight dip from someone else, or it would be way worse yet. It was pretty much the same for everyone. Sadie's dad played slow pitch in the same league with one of the constables who'd caught Mark. Pete Wiens' mother was a part-time secretary at the high school with the wife of the other constable.

Good thing we didn't let Naomi, Joy, or Eleanor come with to the police station. They shouldn't have to confess, we'd decided, because Naomi and Joy didn't really do anything, and Eleanor would probably wet her pants.

Chief Neufeld took us into a room and gave us a scathing lecture, about how stunts like ours wasted their time and tied up valuable resources, and how we were lucky no one got hurt or drowned, and how this sort of foolishness and irresponsibility for sure wasn't what the community expected of its young people, never mind the danger we had put ourselves in. He said he was letting us off with a warning, but he'd better not see us in there again.

"Since you came in on your own, I'm not going to call your parents this time."

We breathed a huge sigh of relief. Apologies flew around the room. But we breathed too soon.

"You'll tell them yourselves," he added. "And believe me, I'll know whether you have or not."

We believed him.

I made up my mind to confess and get it over with. Only my good intentions came to *nusht* because when I got home Dad had gone to work. That made two Saturdays in a row.

There was no way I was telling Beth anything. She'd want to pray over me or something. I felt guilty enough already without that yet. What if Mom found out? She'd be so mortified she'd never show her face out of Eden again. I remembered to feed Tommy, then I went at the siding with my wire brush, scrubbing loose paint like a maniac until I'd scoured every board as high up as I was allowed to go.

Only I was still feeling like I needed to repent. So I let Lena watch *Tarzan* on TV for once, instead of making her watch *American Bandstand*. While she was watching, I picked lettuce for Beth, washed it, and helped her make lunch.

"What's up with you this morning?" Beth asked.

That's what a person gets for trying to be nice.

"If you're hoping to suck up to Dad, don't bother," said Beth. "He had to go into Winnipeg. He won't be home until late."

"I wasn't sucking up. Geez."

Since I was off the hook till tomorrow anyways, one last swim before I got grounded again seemed like a pretty good idea. I made up my mind to stop by Sadie's. I'd tell her I was sorry and that I didn't blame her for being mad at me. I'd be mad at me, too.

I felt better already, after deciding to apologize to Sadie. So I knew it was the right thing to do. First, though, I had to visit Mom. I hadn't gone to see her at all yesterday. I even told Lena she could come with.

At Eden we went for a walk around the grounds again, then played *knippsbrat* a little. I could tell Mom was trying, but she wasn't really into it. When she wasn't looking I checked her eyes to see if it was the real Mom or the robot Mom in charge today, only I couldn't tell.

While we were playing, one of the other patients came and stood over the table, rocking back and forth and watching us. He just stood there, rocking and watching. A thin line of drool ran from the corner of his mouth down his chin, but he didn't wipe it off or anything. I tried not to look, but it was sort of hard not to, with him standing right there. Lena begged me with her eyes to do something.

"Uh, Mom?" I nodded at the guy.

Mom looked up. "Oh, hi Corny," she said, like she didn't mind one bit for him to be standing there drooling.

Corny kept on rocking and watching. Talk about creeping a person out. Lena looked like she might bolt any second. As soon as the first game was finished I told Mom we had to go. She walked us to the door. I don't think she really wanted visitors very much right then anyways, not even Lena and me.

But it wasn't our day. On the way out we were ambushed. A girl was crawling on the floor in the foyer, between us and the door. Her head was hanging down and her arms, her legs, her body, everything was shaking. The girl looked about Beth's age.

"What's wrong with her?" Lena asked, edging as far away as she could.

A nurse appeared. "Don't worry. Sally does this. It'll pass."

Easy for her to say. I took Lena's hand. We followed
Mom, moving slowly around the shaking girl. But then
the girl reached out and grabbed my ankle. My heart
nearly shot right out of my mouth.

"Don't go. Don't leave me," the girl begged.

"There now, Sally." The nurse reached over, took hold
of the girl's arm and pulled it back.

Sally yanked her arm away and went for me again.
Only you bet I backed out of reach real quick.

"Don't leave me!" she wailed.

There wasn't much room to maneuver or for sure I
would've been out of there.

Another person came to help, an orderly I guess. A
doctor waited while the nurse and the orderly just sort of
walked beside the girl, keeping her from bumping into
things.

"Poor Sally," Mom sighed.

The doctor smiled at Lena and me. "Sally didn't mean
to scare you, young ladies."

"I wasn't scared," I denied. Creeped out, I told myself,
which wasn't the same thing as scared. Mostly I just felt
sorry for Sally.

"Girls, this is Dr. Shroeder," Mom said. "These are my
daughters, Elsie and Lena."

"Pleased to meet you." He held out his hand. It felt
cold and limp, like a dead fish.

Someone started wailing in the lounge behind us.

I couldn't take it anymore. Mom didn't belong in this place. I wanted to shout it in that doctor's face. Only of course I didn't. I was way too gutless. "We gotta go," I said. "See you later, Mom." I practically dragged Lena outside.

The fresh air tasted so good I didn't think I'd ever be able to gulp down enough of it. Lena looked back and waved. Probably Mom was standing at the front, waving good-bye. I didn't look.

"I don't like that place," Lena said. "I don't think Mom should be there. She should come home."

"Ya think?" I murmured. A seven year old could see it. It was the idiot doctors who couldn't. Probably they'd been hanging around crazy people so long they didn't know the difference anymore.

❧

The Lord works in mysterious ways, says Reverend Funk. That's an understatement.

I shoved Eden out of my mind and practiced my apology all the way to Sadie's place. When we were almost there already a car turned the corner in front of us and drove away. Sadie's parents were in the front. Sadie, her baby brother, and Jillian sat in the back.

My two best friends were going somewhere together and I wasn't invited.

A few of the gang showed up at the pool – Naomi, Joy, Caleb, and of all people, Mark. Everyone else was probably grounded. I could hardly believe Mark wasn't.

"Dad decided grounding wasn't good enough," Mark explained. "I start work Monday, hoeing beets."

"Youch," Caleb winced.

Ask anyone who has done it. Hoeing beets is like hell on earth. Up at dawn and out in the fields by six. Long hours bent over, sweating in the hot sun until dirt sticks to every bit of you. Dirt in your eyes, dirt in your ears, dirt in your hair, dirt up your nose, and dirt lipstick yet, too. The summer Beth hoed beets she sneezed dirt for weeks. And all the while swarms of mosquitos consider you their personal buffet. All for a whopping buck a row. And I'm not talking your backyard garden rows either.

I couldn't have picked a better way to get even with Mark. I almost felt a bit sorry for him.

"Why did you do it?" I had to ask.

He knew what I meant all right. "I just happened to be there," he shrugged. "Not a big deal."

"For you maybe. I bet Eleanor thinks it was a big deal."

He flushed red. Huh. I wondered if maybe he liked Eleanor. That made a whole lot more sense than to think Mark could just be a nice guy when he wanted.

When I got home after swimming I asked Beth if anyone had called while I was gone, but she said no. So then I called Jillian's house. Maybe I was somehow wrong about my best friends going off together. Jillian's mother said she'd gone with Sadie's family to their cabin at Lake Winnipeg for a couple of days.

If this was God's idea of a joke, I wasn't laughing. He'd answered my prayer all right. Mark wouldn't be around to bug me anymore.

Neither would my best friends.

At bedtime Lena asked if I would read her a story. "Mom always reads me a story."

"I'm too bushed," I told her, rolling around trying to get comfortable. I wasn't in any mood to read to her, even if I knew I should because Mom would want me to, and besides, it would be a nice thing to do for my little sister.

Something hard poked my back. Lena was prodding me with the corner of a book.

"Read me a story or else," she demanded.

"Or else what?"

"Or else I'll tell Dad what you did last night. I heard you talking with your friends."

My own sister. "Give me that." I grabbed the book. It was *Tales from the Arabian Nights*.

Lena jumped into bed and curled up into her pillow. "I want to hear the one about open sesame tonight. Tomorrow you can read the one about the genie in the lamp."

Uy uy uy.

Dear God,

I don't want to seem ungrateful, because I'm really glad that Mark won't be able to pester me for awhile. I don't believe for a minute that this nice guy act he's putting on is going to last.

The thing is, God, nothing has turned out the way I thought it would. Aaron was supposed to like me, not Sadie. Now Sadie hates me, and I think Jillian is on her side. I think maybe I've lost my best friends. I'd rather put up with Mark than lose Jillian and Sadie. So please, if you don't mind, can you help me figure out a way to get things back the way they were? If it's not too much trouble?

I'm trying to understand your will. I guess you probably want me to be happy for Sadie instead of jealous. That's going to be awfully hard, Lord. How can I be happy when I'm so miserable?

Maybe, if you have the time, you could put in a good word for me with Dad, so when I tell him what happened with the police he won't blow his stack completely. Please make Lena keep her mouth shut until I get a chance to tell him.

That's it for now. I know I'm asking an awful lot. If there is only one prayer I can have answered, then my prayer is for Mom to get well so she can come home again. She doesn't belong in Eden.

Probably you'd want me to get myself out of this mess with my friends anyways. But I can't do anything to make Mom better. Even if it's sort of my fault she's there. I need your help to make things right again. Thanks, God.

Amen.

13

A nice day for killing pigs

Trouble follows me closer than my shadow.

Sunday after church I was working up the nerve to tell Dad about our midnight swim. Sunday seemed like a good day to confess. I'd remind Dad what Jesus said about forgiving others.

The sermon that morning had been from Proverbs, about how a "soft answer turns away wrath." Reverend Funk said if we follow Jesus's example and speak to others lovingly and gently instead of with anger, we can calm many storms. I was pretty sure he was thinking about me and Lena when he wrote his sermon.

Anyways, it seemed like good advice to pass on to Dad. He'd stayed home from church to caulk windows and went right back to work again after dinner.

Beth made roast chicken with all the trimmings. Probably because she knew I couldn't eat chicken. Instead I had two helpings of all the trimmings, with extra gravy. Then I changed into grubbies and climbed up on the scaffold beside Dad.

"I don't want you climbing up this high, kidlet," he right away frowned at me.

"I'll be careful." I watched him for a bit, waiting for a good time. "You missed a pretty good sermon." I gave him the Reader's Digest version. "Do you think it works?"

Dad finished squeezing a line of guck to the corner, then smoothed it out with one quick wipe of his finger. If I was doing that, I'd be tempted to lick my finger to see if it maybe tasted like icing.

"I suppose it does. Sometimes. Not always. Some people are too full of anger to hear what anyone else says."

"Well –" I took a deep breath. "I hope this isn't one of those times."

Dad frowned, but I don't know if it was at me or because he wasn't happy with how the caulking looked. I never got to find out.

"We've got company." I nodded toward the street. Mr. and Mrs. Friesen and their two little brats, Mattie and Jonah, piled out of their car. I'd babysat for them once. Once was for sure enough. Besides which, Mr. Friesen may be a deacon in the church and have the biggest house in town and everything, but he was cheap as borscht when it came to paying babysitters.

Dad groaned. "I'm never going to get this job done."

"Do you think we're on some kind of list," I wondered out loud, "and every Sunday someone from church has to come visit us?"

"Be nice," said Dad. But then he grinned and messed up my hair.

We climbed down to meet the Friesens.

"I hope we didn't come at a bad time, Isaak." Mr. Friesen was frowning a little at the caulking gun in Dad's hands. "We didn't expect to find you at work on Sunday afternoon, or we wouldn't have dropped by."

Translation: Dad shouldn't have been working on the Lord's Day. Not that it was any of their business. Except in the Mennonite church, everyone's business was everyone else's business. That's the way it was.

"Doesn't feel like work, not a bit," Dad spoke so soft and gentle I did a double take to see if it was really him talking. He winked at me. "The Lord gave us such a beautiful day, Elsie and I thought we should get out and enjoy it together. Why don't you go on inside? I'll just take a minute to clean up here."

Mrs. Friesen side stepped around Tommy, who was pacing back and forth on the porch. "I'm not overly fond of cats," she sniffed. "I think I have an allergy."

I was thinking that I wasn't overly fond of her when I caught the look Dad gave me over his shoulder. "He doesn't usually hang around this time of day, does he Elsie?"

Oops. I grabbed the empty saucer. Tommy meowed, as if to say, "About time."

Beth showed the Friesens into the house. Of course, yours truly got stuck entertaining the toddlers. Mattie and Jonah followed me outside when I brought Tommy his milk. He lapped it up like he hadn't eaten in a week, but as soon as the first grubby fist went for his tail he was gone.

So then Lena and I herded the boys up to our room and scrounged around in the closet for old toys. Only Mattie had other ideas. He went straight for my model of the lunar landing module.

"Whoaa there!" I scooped up the model, setting it out of reach on top of my dresser. "That's not a toy."

For a little kid Mattie sure knew how to give a dirty look. He opened his mouth, ready to holler.

"Hey, what's this?" I grabbed a stuffed monkey off my bed and shoved it at him. "Look, there's a whole jungle of animals here. You can play Tarzan." I wrapped Lena's baby blanket around his middle for a loincloth.

"Ow!" I heard Lena yelp, only I already had one monster to deal with, so I couldn't check right away to see if everything was okay. Pretty soon though, Mattie was jumping from one bed to the other doing his best Tarzan imitation.

I was pleased with myself. At least until I turned around and there was Jonah yanking books out of the bookcase. One by one he threw them on the floor, making little exploding noises as they landed. Lena was backed almost into the corner, rubbing her arm.

I snatched Jonah's wrist as he went for another book.

"Leggo!" he said. "I'm reading."

"Good for you." I smiled pleasantly. "Only it almost always works best to read one book at a time. You can pick which one."

He picked *How the Elephant Got its Trunk*, which was my favorite ever since Mom read it to me all the time when I was still little. I loved how the words sounded, especially at the beginning when Mom would read in a hushed voice: *In the High and Far-off Times the Elephant, O Best Beloved, had no trunk.* I loved that the Elephant's child was full of "'satiable curtiosity" and got in trouble all the time.

The kid had good taste anyways. I sat him on the floor, pulled Lena down beside him and told her to read. Then I started putting back the rest of the books. All of a sudden I didn't hear Tarzan anymore. Mattie had disappeared.

Lena paused.

"Read!" I told her, and went in search of the missing ape-man. I found him in Beth's room. He'd shed his loin-cloth and was trying on a bra he'd pulled from her dresser drawer.

"I know what those are," he announced, pointing at my chest.

"You do, do you?" Right away when I opened my mouth I knew I'd made a mistake.

"Boobs!" The little pervert grinned.

I choked. So much for Beth's theory that I didn't have anything a guy would notice. Too bad the guy was a five year old.

"That's it. Come here once. Let's get that thing off you. Bras are for girls, not boys." *Soft and gentle, soft and gentle*, I reminded myself.

Mattie turned stubborn. "I'm playing dress up."

"Nope," I said cheerfully. Calmly. "N-O. *Nay*. No way. Not going to happen. Beth would skin us both alive."

Mattie hugged himself to keep me from getting at the bra. Unless I got rough I wasn't going to get it off him. Time to try something else. "Have it your way." I stepped back as if I didn't care, shrugging my shoulders. "Makes me no never mind if you grow up to be a girl."

"I'm a boy!" he shouted.

"Well, I'll tell you a secret, if you promise not to tell anyone. Not ever." I was whispering now, and looking over my shoulder like I was making sure no one else could hear. "See, the thing is," I paused for effect. "I used to be a boy, too." I threw up my hands to show I was powerless to stop the disaster. "If it happened to me, it could happen to you, not?"

His eyes grew wide. He whipped off the bra and threw it on the ground.

"Whew! You're safe." I scooped up Beth's underwear and returned it to the drawer before the kid got wise to me.

"I don't like you." He aimed a squint-eyed death stare at me.

"That's okay. The feeling's mutual. But this is my house, and if you're going to visit you have to do what I say. So there."

"I didn't want to come here. My mom made me."

"Moms will do that."

"My mom says you and your sister run wild all over town. She says, she says you're a couple of . . . of ragamuffins."

"Figures." I was pretty proud of the way I'd kept my cool until then. "What else does she say?"

"She says she feels sorry for you, 'cause you don't got a mother at home to teach you –"

Calm and gentle, my heinie. I grabbed the kid's arm and yanked him to his feet. "Yeah, well, your mother's a liar. You should try telling her to mind her own beeswax for once."

Judging by the horror on his face you'd have thought I'd just told him there was no Santa Claus. He let out a wail and headed for the door, hollering for Mommy.

A shriek from my bedroom drowned him out. Jumping Jehoshaphat. It didn't sound like things were going much better for Lena. I hurried back, *schlaping* Mattie along.

"H-he-he –" Lena couldn't spit out the words. She looked ready to strangle Jonah. The little twirp was

waving something in his grubby fist. My stomach did a
nosedive. He was waving a torn page with a crocodile
pulling on the elephant's trunk.

"You, you –!" The only words that came to mind I
couldn't say in front of a kid. "You little toad!" I managed
to choke out before grabbing his wrist. I half-carried,
half-dragged both of them down the stairs, Lena trotting
along behind. Their chubby little legs barely touched the
ground until I plopped them on the living room floor
beside their mother.

Mrs. Friesen frowned. "What in heaven's name –?"

"These two want to go home," I said.

"Elsie, what do you think –"

"Sorry, Dad. Lena and I are off to run wild around
town. C'mon, Lena."

I pedaled furiously for a good five blocks before I
stopped seething enough to let go of the handlebars.
Seething was another good word, I decided. I'd have to
remember it, especially if we were going to get a whole
pile more visitors while Mom was sick.

I made two blocks with no hands easy. I wished I'd
never have to see those little fiends again. Pretty good
chance of that wish coming true. The Friesens for sure
wouldn't be back for a while. One by one I was scaring off
the whole church membership.

Three blocks. I wished Mattie and Jonah would come
down with mumps. It was possible. I'd heard it was going
around. I was doing them a favor really. Somewhere I'd

heard it was supposed to be better for boys to get mumps when they were little, not?

Four blocks. I wished Jillian and Sadie would like me again. There was some hope for that, maybe. If I found a way to make things up with Sadie.

Five blocks. I wished I could turn around and go home and Mom would be there.

Fat chance. I grabbed the handlebars because I couldn't stop the stupid tears filling my eyes and I couldn't see right. *Fuy.* I pulled over and wiped my face with the back of my hand. Lena caught up to me.

"Are we going to visit Mom?" she asked.

"Sure. Why not."

Sunday afternoon was why not. I hadn't thought about how many visitors there would be on a Sunday afternoon. The lounge was crowded with all the people, and still more people I didn't know even were in Mom's room. Practically all of them looked at us funny, not laughing funny, but funny like they felt sorry for us. We got out of there in a hurry, let me tell you, without stopping to see Mom.

Then we ran wild around town some more yet, until I was good and sure the Friesens would be gone. When we got home Dad was watching *Hymn Sing*, which usually put him in a pretty good mood. Except not today.

"*Nah yo,*" he said, pointing to the stairs, which meant for me to get myself to my room. "This was sure a nice day for killing pigs, thanks to you."

No one cared less about my side of the story. My essay on How I Spent My Summer Vacation was going to be easy to write this year. One word would do it. Grounded.

Now was not a good time to make Dad still madder, so I kept my mouth shut about the midnight swim.

Lena picked up the torn page with the elephant's trunk ripped in half and tried to smooth it out. "I'm sorry your book got ripped up."

She looked miserable, more miserable than me even. I slid to the floor beside her. "Maybe we can fix it."

I tried fitting the torn piece to the page. "Lookit, we can tape it."

"I'll go ask Beth for tape." Lena jumped up. Without warning she threw her arms around my neck. "Don't worry. I won't tell on you, Elsie. Even if you don't read to me anymore."

I was so surprised I hugged her back. "I don't mind reading to you," I said.

Then she ran downstairs and even if I thought I was over crying about it I guess I wasn't, because just like that for no good reason, the tears were pouring down my face all over again. It was stupid, stupid, stupid to cry. It was just a little kid's book anyways. Only I'd been praying all the time for seven days now and things were getting worse. If Mom was here she'd fix everything. She'd make everything all right again. She wouldn't let Dad send me to my room for something that wasn't my fault, or let

Beth boss me around. She'd know what to do about Jillian and Sadie, too.

But Mom wasn't any closer to coming home than before.

I was sick of being grounded all the time.

I was sick of telling God I was sorry and asking for forgiveness.

I was terrible hungry for a hamburger.

And my legs were itching me like crazy because the hair was growing back all prickly, just like Jillian said. Dad was right about one thing; it was a nice day for killing pigs all right.

Two weeks to go still. That seemed like forever.

❧

Dear God,

I've had a lousy day. I don't even want to go into it.

All this praying is supposed to help me understand your will, but there are more and more things that I don't understand one bit. My book is ruined! Dad's all mad at me again, my friends are gone, and nothing is going right.

Please, God, make my mom well again. Please let her come home. I'm really trying my best, God.

I hope you don't mind me saying it, but sometimes I think you're lying down on the job, God.

Amen.

14

He knows from where the wind blows

First thing in the morning before he left for work, Dad got me started painting the garage. He showed me how to stir the paint, how to take the right amount and not too much on my brush or roller, and how to work in a wide band from one side of the scaffold to the other, starting at the top. The top of where I was working anyways, since Dad wouldn't let me go all the way up to the top of the house.

"Think you can handle it? Without starting a third world war, that is." He was still pretty steamed yet about yesterday.

"I can handle it," I muttered.

"Good. Because I'm late for work." He filled the paint tray for me and set the can of paint on the ground. "Where are the rags?"

"On the porch."

"Do you think you could get me one, or is that too much to ask?" he grumbled, turning and looking for a place to set the paint tray.

Jumping Jehoshaphat. If what he wanted was for me to hand him a rag, then that's what he should've asked for. I jumped off the scaffold to grab one.

It wasn't my fault I didn't see Tom-cat sneaking up behind me. It wasn't my fault he got spooked when I jumped, and scooted off. And it wasn't my fault Tommy scooted right under Dad's feet, at the same time Dad turned to set the paint tray down on the scaffold.

And for sure it wasn't my fault that Dad's foot came down right on Tommy's tail. One thing about Dad, he's no lightweight. Poor Tom let out a howl loud enough to wake the dead.

Dad tried to dodge Tommy, but that was sort of hard to do with a wet paintbrush in one hand and a full paint tray in the other. He dropped the tray on the scaffold platform and sidestepped, cursing under his breath.

Only problem was, Tommy dodged in the same direction. Dad's other foot came down on his paw. Tommy let loose another howl. Dad jumped straight up and Tommy darted out from under.

Everything might have been okay still, if Dad hadn't tried to kick him as he streaked away.

"Scram!" he snarled.

"Don't hurt him!" I yelled. But there was no chance of that. Tommy was gone.

For a split second, Dad didn't have any feet on the ground at all. His arms flew back as he tried to get his balance. One hand hit the paint tray, which was sticking off the edge of the scaffold. The tray flipped up and over. Paint launched itself straight at him. I could see that Dad was going to go down and there was absolutely nothing I could do about it. He almost saved himself; one hand found a corner of the porch landing. Only then his hand slipped and he crashed onto the steps, landing hard on his wrist. Dad groaned, tilted, and then rolled the rest of the way down.

On the first roll he banged his shin. On the next roll he scraped his back, then he bounced hard on his keister before landing on the sidewalk.

Uy uy uy. I didn't move. I didn't breathe even. And for sure I didn't so much as think about laughing.

Dad let loose a sizzling stream of Plautdietsch that didn't need any translating.

"*Isaak! Schauntboa!*" Grandma stood on the sidewalk, horrified.

Dad got to his feet, which wasn't easy because he wasn't moving too well and was holding his wrist. I tried to help him but he brushed me off. He didn't say a word, just stood there with his eyes blazing, first at Grandma, then at me. I could practically see the steam coming off him. Grandma *harumphed*, turned on her heel, and deserted me.

Dad looked at me. His mouth moved, but no words came out.

Finally, he spluttered, "Don't hurt *him*?!" Then he turned and limped inside.

Tommy didn't show himself at all for the rest of the day. He knew from where the wind blew.

So did I. I painted all day, not just in the morning. I never stopped working to go for a swim even. The first coat on the garage was done before supper.

Probably, I thought, it was a good idea if I wasn't around when Dad came home. I grabbed something to eat and went for a bike ride. Only there was nowhere for me to go. Jillian and Sadie weren't home yet.

For a while I practiced riding with no hands. On my first try a truck forced me to the side of the road, practically into the curb. I hadn't even gone a block. On the next try I wasn't sitting right and couldn't get my balance at all. I tried a third time. I never saw the hole in the pavement until it was too late. I grabbed on to save myself, just before my tires hit the hole with such a jolt I bit my tongue yet on top of it all.

Three strikes. I was out. It was a stupid game anyways.

At home, Dad was sitting at the kitchen table, his back to the door, eating supper with one hand. His other arm was in a sling, the wrist wrapped tightly.

I wanted to ask if he was all right. I wanted to say I was sorry, even if I wasn't sure for what, exactly.

"I'm going to bed," I mumbled, and went up to my room to read.

After a while, Dad took off. Probably he was going to

visit Mom. I crept downstairs and put out a can of tuna for Tommy, so he'd know we didn't mean to scare him. For once Beth never made a fuss about wasting good tuna on an alley cat. She told me Dad had sprained his wrist.

"Don't worry," she said. "He'll get over it."

"Yeah," I said. "Next year maybe."

It didn't hardly cool off at all that night. The house was stuffy and hot. Way too hot to sleep, that's for sure. I kicked off my blankets and the sheet and lay there suffocating and listening to the night and hoping I might hear a couple of cats going at it because then at least I'd know Tommy was back and defending his turf.

Only I guess it was too hot even for stray cats to bother fighting.

❧

Dear God,

Thank you for not letting Dad or Tommy get too badly hurt this morning.

I'm sorry for what happened, even though it wasn't really my fault. It was an accident. How come Dad has to get so mad when it was just an accident?

Sometimes, he's the one who makes me mad.

Please help Dad cool off and stop being so grumpy all the time.

And please take care of Mom. Help her get well again. We all need her here at home. That's an understatement.

Amen.

15

Weak like a dishrag

They wouldn't let me see my mom today.

I didn't tell anyone I was going to visit. I didn't know myself until I went. One minute I was starting to paint a second coat on the garage, and thinking about how this morning Dad was talking to me in one-word sentences still. Then I got to wondering about Mom.

I hadn't gone to see her for a couple of days. At breakfast this morning Dad hadn't said how she was doing. I wondered if maybe I should go check if she was all right. Then my chest got tight and my heart started going a mile a minute and then, out of the blue, for no good reason, I felt like crying some more.

Holy Moses. These days it was like I'd turned on a fountain and couldn't shut it off again. The next minute I'd dumped my paintbrush in the thinner, shoved the lid on the paint can, and was racing over to Eden on my bike.

When I got there it was almost nine o'clock. The front doors were locked, but a nurse at the reception desk buzzed me in.

She wouldn't let me see Mom. I was too early for visiting hours, she said. "Your mother had a treatment this morning. She's resting. You mustn't disturb her."

She didn't tell me what kind of treatment, and I didn't have the guts to ask. She probably wouldn't have told me. It was probably one of those things no one would tell me because I was supposed to be too young to understand.

The nurse looked at me over top of her glasses like grown-ups do when you're bugging them. "You can come back during regular visiting hours this afternoon."

I turned to leave. Only when I shoved on the door it wouldn't open. I shoved again, then I tried yanking it open. I shoved and yanked and shoved and yanked and still the stupid door wouldn't budge. I was starting to get pretty mad over everything.

"Take it easy, young lady. I haven't unlocked the doors yet this morning," the nurse said. She took her time walking over to punch some numbers into a little box on the wall beside the door.

The damn doors were locked from the inside, too!

They wouldn't let me see my mom. She was locked in like a prisoner! Right away I started thinking of ways to rescue her. Which even if I knew was pretty stupid, I couldn't help thinking. I couldn't help thinking that God didn't seem to be in any hurry to answer my prayers. I stood in the warm sunshine, but I didn't feel one bit warm. I was shivering like crazy.

One thing for sure, I wasn't leaving until I knew Mom was okay. *What would Nancy Drew or the Hardy Boys do?* I wondered. *They'd sneak into the building somehow.*

I strolled around the back of Mom's wing, trying to look casual, but all the time I was counting windows until I found the one I thought was her room. The curtains were drawn tight. Even when I shoved in between the shrubs to press my face to the glass I couldn't find a crack to see through.

Anyways, the windows in her room weren't like regular windows that opened. The bottom part was one big pane of glass. On top of that was a smaller section that opened. Too high to reach. Too small to climb through. And right now it was shut tight.

Fuy. Mom should have fresh air. Someone should make sure she had fresh air at least.

"Hey kid."

Jumping Jehoshaphat. My heart catapulted me out of the bushes and back onto the sidewalk. Now what? An orderly stood by the open door at the end of the wing, watching me. He lit a smoke and tossed the match in the shrub bed. "Can I help you?"

"No thanks." I strolled past him and around the corner, then started to run.

Talk about a weak-kneed, yellow-bellied, gutless wonder. *Schvack aus en tubbdook,* I could hear Dad saying. Weak like a dishrag. Would Nancy Drew give up at the first sign of trouble? *No way*, I told myself. *Don't be such a dishrag.*

Instead of riding away I circled around behind the grounds, riding along the floodway. I left my bike tucked under a tree and snuck back to peek around the corner. The orderly was gone.

If people came out here to smoke, I thought, then maybe . . .

Before I could think too much about it, I ran across the lawn and pulled on the door. Sure enough, it was unlocked. I slipped inside. It was that easy.

My bare feet never made a sound as I tiptoed down the hall. Beth would throw a fit if she knew I didn't even have any shoes on. Then I had to laugh at myself for thinking like that, because no shoes would be the least of my problems if I was caught.

Lots of the doors I passed were open. But either the rooms were empty, or else the people inside never took any notice of me. A few doors were closed, like Mom's. There it was.

This detective stuff was a cinch. Holding my breath, I pushed open the door, just a crack. The room was dim, but not really dark. Even with the curtains drawn tight some light got through. It was stuffy, though. I could feel the stuffiness leaking out, smothering me.

"Mom?" I whispered. Screwing up my courage I pushed the door open a bit more, just enough to slip inside. I gently shut the door behind me. For a while I stood there, watching and listening to Mom's deep, slow breathing. Why was she sleeping in the middle of the morning? Should I wake her up?

"Mom?" I repeated, quietly. No answer. Probably I should let her sleep, I decided. She'd had a treatment, the nurse had said. I didn't know what that meant, but it was a good bet that whatever it was made her tired. Now that I knew she was all right – sort of anyways – I could leave.

Only first I'd open her window. I crept on tiptoe across the room, quietly picked up the chair from beside her bed, and set it down by the window. Standing on the chair, I pushed the curtain back just enough to reach the latch.

The breath of fresh air was warm already, but it tasted delicious. I let the curtain fall again. It moved a little bit with the breeze.

Before leaving, I leaned over Mom, studying her face. Whatever they were doing didn't look like it had made a difference. She looked tired, the same as always. "See you later, Mom," I whispered.

I slipped out the door, turning to close it, being ever so careful not to wake Mom. The door clicked shut about half a second before my arm was practically yanked out of its socket.

"What do you think you're doing in here!" The nurse's voice was hushed, but she was plenty mad. Funny thing was, she sounded far away all of sudden behind this crazy ringing in my ears.

This nurse wasn't the same one at the front desk. Whoever she was, she had a grip like King Kong. She hauled me out of the patient's wing, past reception, and right to an office nearby, never shutting up once. I didn't hear a word she said though. I wondered when the ringing in my ears had started.

"Dr. Shroeder?" She knocked on the open office door. "Sorry to disturb you, but I found this youngster sneaking into patients' rooms. Should I call the police?"

Finally my tongue came unglued. "I wasn't sneaking into people's rooms!" I shook off the nurse's hand.

"No, no." The doctor got up and walked around his desk. "I'm sure that won't be necessary." His voice echoed. He loomed over me, smiling this great big fake smile. "I'm sure the young lady has an explanation."

Young lady. Who was he kidding? I put my arms behind my back, hiding the streaks of paint I hadn't stopped to wash off. There wasn't much I could do about my bare feet. Besides, he didn't remember me even. I wasn't sure whether to be relieved or mad about that.

The front desk nurse decided to put in her two cents worth. She stuck her head in the door. "I told her she wasn't allowed to visit her mother this morning. I don't know how she got back in."

I wasn't about to tell them. I shook my head, slapping it against my hand to try and clear the ringing in my ears, like I did when there was water in them after swimming. Probably I looked like a nutcase.

Dr. Shroeder raised his eyebrows. "Her mother?" He still hadn't figured it out.

"That's Esther Redekop's daughter," the nurse said.

"Ahh." Now he remembered. "It's Elsie, right? What's going on, Elsie?"

Something inside me snapped, like a great big elastic band that was pulled so tight it couldn't be pulled any more so it just – snapped.

"You've got no right keeping my mother here. She's not crazy, you know!" My voice sounded strange.

"No one said she was crazy."

"She doesn't belong here! If you think she belongs here, then you're the crazy ones!"

Halfway through the ringing in my ears stopped and I knew I'd been shouting. I swallowed. I didn't see any good reason to stick around to hear what they had to say. It wouldn't make a diff, anyways. I ducked around the nurse and tore out the door, running like the wind all the way around the building to get my bike.

I cut through a few back alleys and across the school yard yet, too, just to make sure I wasn't being followed. Then I had to laugh at myself. This was Hopefield. They'd probably be waiting at my back door when I got home, ready to take me away.

Huge, billowing clouds towered over the town. A thunderstorm was on its way, at least I hoped so. Rain would be a relief.

"Where did you disappear to?" Beth asked when I walked in the kitchen.

I was puffing pretty hard still from racing all the way home. I needed a drink. "Riding my bike," I said, heading for the fridge. That was the truth. One thing I'd figured out was that it was easier to lie if I stuck as close to the truth as possible. Now I just had to distract Beth from digging any deeper.

"Have you seen Tommy? He wasn't around this morning." I poured myself some Kool-Aid and started gulping it down.

"No, I haven't seen that disgusting furball. Thank goodness for small miracles." Beth was tearing lettuce for a salad. A plate of tuna sandwiches was sitting on the table.

I hoped nothing bad had happened to Tommy – that Dad had scared him away for good or he'd met his match in an alley fight or been hit by a car or something. A horrible feeling squeezed at my gut as I sat down and put a sandwich on my plate, staring at it. I couldn't eat it like that; I'd have to scrape out the tuna.

I just didn't know what to do. Not about Tommy, or Mom.

"Wash up at least."

It was useless talking to Beth. I shoved back from the table and went to wash my hands.

"Satisfied?" I shoved my freshly scrubbed hands in Beth's face as I pushed by her.

"Philistine," Beth muttered.

At supper that evening Dad said he'd got a call from Eden about me. "Did you really tell Dr. Shroeder that Mom shouldn't be there?"

"Well she shouldn't."

Dad sighed. He adjusted the sling around his arm, wincing. "You don't know what the doctors are doing for Mom. You can't just walk in there any time you please."

Here was my chance. All I had to do was say, "Then tell me what they're doing."

"I didn't hurt anything," I said. "I opened Mom's window. It was closed and her room was like a tomb in there so I opened her window. What's the big deal?"

I expected him to yell or something. I expected him to maybe slam his fist on the table and tell me to smarten up, that I was too old to act so childish. I expected him to tell me that I was grounded again. I was ready for it.

He didn't do any of those things. "There's no big deal, kidlet," he said, shaking his head. "Sometimes I wonder if she should be in there, too."

That's the one thing I didn't expect him to say. "I'm sorry you hurt your wrist," I blurted.

It was after supper, when Auntie Nettie stopped by and she and Dad were downstairs talking, that I got an answer to the question I'd never asked. Part of an answer anyways. The grown-ups thought I was outside, but I snuck upstairs and listened by the air register.

At first they talked mostly in Plautdietsch and I was just about ready to give up. And then I heard Dad's rumbly voice say in English, "The headaches are worse than ever."

Auntie Nettie answered, "*Ach*." I could almost see her shaking her head. "That's what the shock treatments do, not?"

The stupid hot tears started pouring out of me again. I didn't even know why I was crying.

For once I wished I'd kept my big nose out of it.

❧

Dear God,

What are they doing to Mom in that place? What are shock treatments? Is that why she was sleeping in the middle of the morning? She could do that at home.

They're supposed to be making her better, but I don't think they are. I really think they need your help, God. I don't mean to be pushy, but are you going to get around to helping Mom soon?

I guess I should say I'm sorry for swearing so much today, even if it was mostly in my head. Only I don't feel very sorry.

Amen.

❧

I didn't feel much like praying tonight. I didn't feel much like sleeping either. My mind was still too wide awake yet, wide awake and thinking about shock treatments.

Were they trying to shock Mom out of being sad? How did you do something like that?

Maybe you could tell a shocking story, one that was really scary. Or wait until a person came around a corner and jump out at them, yelling. Or dump a pail of cold water on them when they opened a door.

I kept thinking over and over again of all the ways to shock a person.

That way I didn't have to think about the one way that made me want to throw up.

16

Not a person to eat noodles with

The day started out top-of-the-summer hot. And then got hotter.

I'm talking road-melting-in-front-of-you hot. Can't-walk-barefoot-on-the-pavement hot. Bike-tires-sink-into-the-asphalt hot. The kind of hot where you get out of the pool to suntan but in two minutes your skin is burning and you have to jump in the water again. The kind of sticky, wilty, dripping hot where you lie in bed at night with no covers, wearing nothing but underwear and still stick to the sheets.

Pray-for-a-thunderstorm hot.

Dad said I should take a few days off until it was more bearable again. But I painted for a couple of hours early in the morning anyways, because what else was there to do and because I liked painting.

First thing after lunch, Lena and I went looking for Tommy. We checked up and down the alley on our way to the pool. We checked between the stacks in the lumber-yard at the end of the block where Tommy sometimes liked to hang out. We even walked along the railway tracks, checking to see if he was hiding out in the ditches maybe.

"I bet he found a girlfriend, or some old lady who likes cats," I said. "He'll be back. He takes off like this all the time, not?"

Lena chewed on her lower lip, a sure sign she was worried. I wiped the sweat off my face. Right now all I wanted was to go for a swim.

The pool was crowded already by the time we got there. Even the parking lot was full. Lena grabbed the one empty spot in the bike racks and ran off to find her friends. It took me a while to find enough room for my bike. I was wedging it into place when a shrill, angry voice close by nearly made me jump out of my skin.

"You just come along with me! Right this instant."

There was Mrs. Friesen maybe a dozen steps up the slope, coming around the corner of the fence and headed my way. I ducked behind my bike, like I was fixing the chain or something.

"Don't you try playing dumb with me, young man. I saw you take my son's money."

Curiosity got the best of me. I lifted my head just enough to peer over top of my bike seat. One look at Mrs.

Friesen was enough to make a person fall to their knees and pray for salvation on the spot. She was hauling a scrawny, half-naked Mexican kid by the wrist. The kid's eyes were ready to pop right out of their sockets. Mattie and Jonah were hiding behind their mom.

A trickle of sweat tickled as it ran down the middle of my chest.

"Hand it over," Mrs. Friesen demanded. She held out one hand, waiting, never letting go of the kid's wrist with the other.

"I-I find da money, lady. Yust dere." The kid pointed beside the sidewalk and stuttered something in Plaut-dietsch.

"You know very well my son dropped it," she said. "Taking money that doesn't belong to you is stealing. Stealing is a terrible sin. People who steal go to jail."

Terrified, the kid dug in his pocket with his free hand. He fished out some change and held it out. Mrs. Friesen grabbed it. But she didn't let him go. She stayed clamped down on his wrist and gave it to him still more, about how God had seen what he did and how he must ask for forgiveness or God would make sure that he was punished.

The boy mumbled something in Low German again. He was so petrified he probably forgot how to speak English. Probably he belonged to one of the Mexican Mennonite families that came up to work in the fields every summer.

The look he was giving the kids in the pool pretty much said it all. It was a blistering hot day and he wanted to go swimming. Only he didn't have a quarter to get in. I bet he thought it was his lucky day when he saw that money lying in the grass. But instead of a nice dip in the pool, he'd got Mrs. Friesen threatening him with eternal damnation.

"I never steal nothing," the boy pleaded, trying to pull away. "Please, lady."

Mrs. Friesen shook him a little. "Didn't steal it, indeed. Don't let me catch you near my boys, again. Is that clear?"

The second Mrs. Friesen let go of his wrist, the kid tore off. I heard a truck start up, and then a dirty, battered pick-up pulled out of the parking lot and headed down the park road behind me. For some reason I ducked deeper into the row of bikes. By now my legs were all pins and needles. They needed to stand up already but I had to stay scrunched behind my bike while Mrs. Friesen fussed over her monsters yet, warning them to stay away from boys like that. Finally they headed to the pool. It seemed like forever but the whole thing probably only took a couple of minutes.

No big deal. Except . . .

One time I watched my cousin skinning some mink that he'd trapped. First thing he cut up the mink's back legs to its tail, working the fur off. Then he hung the mink up by its back feet and just sort of sliced here and sliced there and then peeled the pelt back whole, like taking off a sock inside out. The skin came away that easy, too.

I felt like I was that mink, watching Mrs. Friesen – who sat up front in church every Sunday and taught Sunday School and everything – watching her chew up and spit out that little kid who only wanted to go for a swim. Like I was the one turned inside out.

I was still feeling sick about it when Jillian and Sadie showed up at the pool together, pretending nothing had changed. Only they laid out their towels with Aaron and Pete on either side. So then I made myself into a robot like Mom, a robot that found a spot to suntan beside Joy, and smiled brightly at Jillian and Sadie while they talked about what a great time they'd had at the lake. I could pretend nothing had changed, too.

Even if everything had changed.

My best friends were now best friends with each other and there wasn't a thing I could do about it. I wanted Aaron to like me but he didn't. I wished Mark didn't like me but maybe he did.

In school last year my teacher, Miss Gerbrandt, caught me passing a note to Aaron one time. It wasn't about anything, and it wasn't like I was the only one who was passing notes, but I was the one who got caught. She sent me to stand in the hall, then came out and told me I was way too young to be thinking about such things as boys.

"I don't want any more of this nonsense in class, understand?" she said.

How can a person be too young to think about boys? If you're thinking about them, then you're thinking about them. A person doesn't go looking for thoughts like that. The thoughts are just there, in your head. You think what you think.

If I could stop thoughts like that I would because they send messages to other parts of a person's body and make a person feel weird. Which is okay I guess, if the person you like likes you back. But for sure it isn't so nice if he doesn't.

Jillian and Sadie hadn't been grounded. Maybe they hadn't told their parents even. I hadn't told Dad yet. Now that I'd waited this long, I figured I might as well not bother. Maybe he wouldn't find out. Except not saying anything was sort of like lying and lying was definitely a sin. Especially when you were lying to your parents. That was like breaking two commandments at once.

My list of sins was getting pretty long. Lying, stealing, being jealous, fighting, swearing, thinking impure thoughts. No wonder God wasn't answering my prayers.

And now there was this. What I'd seen in the park didn't seem right. I couldn't make it fit with what we learned in Sunday School. If a Christian wasn't always a good person, did that mean good people weren't always Christians?

Reverend Funk says God is love. But then the reverend and even the Bible say that to be saved from eternal hell a person has to accept the Lord Jesus Christ as their savior.

Even in Hopefield I knew that not everyone believed

in God the same way Mennonites did. I knew about Jews and Muslims and Hindus and Buddhists and Catholics. Were all the people who believed differently going to hell? Did everyone have a different God, or were they all the same God with different names? What made Mennonites right and everyone else wrong?

What about people who didn't believe in God at all?

Would God really damn people to hell – even if they were good people like say, Ghandi – just because they maybe grew up believing something else?

I was suddenly shivery inside and out even if the temperature was over ninety degrees already. A terrible thought crept into the back of my mind. It was so terrible I pushed it back out before I could finish thinking it even.

A thunderstorm grumbled all around us most of the afternoon, but it never got close enough for the life-guards to make us get out of the pool. I wished it would rain, a real downpour, and scrub the whole world clean like it did for Noah.

Conditions favored it, but instead the storm blew around us.

≫

Dear God,

There's a lot to talk to you about, so much that I don't know where to start. First thing, though, I'm sorry I've been mad at you the last couple of nights.

Beth and Lena and I still fight sometimes. When you miss someone so much like we miss Mom, even when you try to understand why that someone isn't there, you really don't. And it makes you feel kind of crabby so then you have to be mad at something and usually it's pretty easy to be mad at your sisters.

Dad's wrist is almost better. And he was so happy with how good the garage looked he said I could paint the house, too, if I wanted. So if you had something to do with that, thanks.

I don't know what to think about Mrs. Friesen. I know it's wrong to steal and everything. Still, I'm pretty sure Mrs. Friesen didn't act like a good Christian today. At least she didn't speak softly or with love. I didn't hear too much forgiveness in her voice. It's just that she's supposed to be a good church member and everything, but for sure she isn't a person to eat noodles with.

I'm sorry for having such bad thoughts about people. I know Jesus said, "Let he who is without sin cast the first stone," and that's not me. I guess Christians make mistakes, too. I don't know why it bothers me so much, about that boy. It just does.

One thing I know, Mom would've given him the money so he could go swimming. She'd probably have bought him an ice cream to boot.

Mom almost seemed a little better when I went to see her today, except she had a bit of a headache. Maybe they gave her another treatment this morning.

Please take care of Mom, God. And help me to understand how it could be your will for her to be sick. If you make Mom better I won't even care that Jillian and Sadie hate me. Well, maybe I'll care, but I'll try not to.

One more thing. Please take care of Tommy, wherever he is. I'm a little worried about him.

Maybe, if it's not too much trouble, you could give me a sign of some kind so I'd know you were listening.

Amen.

17

His tree is missing a few leaves

ad gave Tommy away.

I didn't find out even until this morning, after Tommy had been gone four days already. I might not have found out at all except I told Dad I wasn't going to paint that morning so I could look for Tommy instead.

Dad looked confused. "I told you already, you don't need to worry about that old tom anymore. He's living the high life with a farmer north of town."

Only he hadn't told us already. Four days, and this was the first he'd said about it. He'd forgot. It wasn't like he was trying to keep it a secret or anything. He'd just forgot.

Honest to God, I think he was surprised when Lena started to cry.

"*Nah meyahles*, simmer down. There's no reason to get yourselves all worked up over it. Tommy's better off in a barn with other cats. There are plenty of mice to chase. It's warm in the winter."

My whole body was shaking, I was so mad. I couldn't speak, I was so mad.

"Jumping Jehoshaphat! Would someone please tell me what all the fuss is about?" Dad said. "Most days you can't even remember to feed it!"

"His name is Tommy!" I said. Lena crawled under the table to cry her eyes out.

"It's not like I took it out and shot it. I was doing the damn cat a favor, giving it to Nickel Enns." Dad shook his head. "I'm going to work."

Figures, I thought. The kitchen was pretty quiet after he left. Beth handed Lena a bowl of cereal and let her eat it under the table.

"Dad's right, *schnigglefritz*," she said. "Tommy's better off on a farm. He was filthy and probably full of fleas and worms and who knows what else?"

"As if." I gave her a withering glare as I shoved my chair back from the table. "You knew. You're just as much to blame."

"*Vite dee!*" she snapped. She had to be pretty pissed off to talk Plautdietsch. "I've had it to here with your lousy attitude. You're the one who couldn't be bothered to put out a bowl of milk half the time."

I stomped outside. I went into the garden and there were no ripe tomatoes yet but I yanked a green tomato off and threw it as hard as I could against a hydro pole.

And all the time I was swearing under my breath, calling Dad every dirty name I could think of in both English and Plautdietsch.

The worst thing was, Dad and Beth were right. I'd done a lousy job of looking out for Tommy and now he was gone and it was mostly my fault. What would Mom say when she got home? It wasn't enough that I'd got her all upset in the first place so she had to go to Eden, now I'd messed up the one thing she'd asked me to do yet.

I tried painting for awhile, even though it was going to be too devilish hot again to paint for long and my heart really wasn't in it.

So I painted Tommy's name over and over again with the creamy siding paint, smoothing it over each time before moving on to the next board. Every time I smoothed it out it hurt, like he was gone all over again.

Lena came outside and hung around, watching me. I could feel her eyes on my back while I painted, which bugged me and made me want to turn around and slap her.

"Can I do that, too?" she whined.

"No. You're too little."

"Please? I want to paint Tommy's name, too."

"Go play next door."

"No one's home. Pretty please? With sugar on it?"

I gritted my teeth. "I said no. Why don't you just get lost once?"

"I hate you."

"I don't give a care."

She threw something at me, a clump of dirt from the garden. She missed by a mile, but the dirt hit the siding that I'd just finished painting.

"Now look what you've done!" I pounced, grabbing her shirt before she could escape. "Clean it up."

"Make me."

That did it. I wrestled her to the ground and sat on her, pinning her arms with my knees. I didn't plan to hurt her or anything. There was a better way to teach her a lesson. "Just remember, you asked for it."

Flicking my middle finger against my thumb, I *knippsed* her nose, like I was playing *knippsbrat* only hitting her nose instead of a disc. Not hard. Just enough to sting a bit. Just enough to drive her crazy. *Knippse, knippse, knippse.*

She shook her head from side to side, but then I just squeezed my knees against her head so she couldn't move.

"Let go!" she screamed.

Knippse, knippse, knippse.

"*Pppleaase,*" she started to sob. "I'll clean it up already."

Knippse, knippse, knippse. Only I was more gentle now, because I was starting to feel sorry for her. "Promise?"

"I promise."

I let her go, keeping a good grip on one arm in case she tried to run away. But she took the rag I gave her and started to wipe off the mess on the siding, still sniffling.

"You missed a spot," I pointed with my paintbrush.

Lena turned her head to see where I was pointing and

my paintbrush dabbed the tip of her nose. It was an accident, but I half-expected her to throw a spaz anyways. Instead she started to laugh. "That tickled. Do it again."

Why not? I dabbed polka dots on both her cheeks. Then I painted a triangle on her forehead and two lines across her chin.

"Do more!" she squealed. "Let me do you!"

In no time we'd decorated our faces, arms, and legs with polka dots, stripes, and anything else we could think of, laughing ourselves silly the whole time.

When Beth came outside to see what was going on, we were sitting on the grass painting our toenails and laughing ourselves nearly dead.

That was the end of that.

While we were cleaning up, Lena out of the blue said, "I know what we could do."

She had a paint smudge still across one cheek. I found a clean spot on the rag and scrubbed it off for her. "What's that?"

"We could go get Tommy back." She was dead serious.

"We don't know where the farm is," I reminded her.

She looked so terrible sad I couldn't bear it. "It would be a good idea though," I added, "if we knew."

Lena tried to smile. "Yeah."

Really, for a little sister, half the time she wasn't so bad.

❧

First thing when we got to the pool, Lena dragged me out of the change room. "You have to watch if I can swim my widths," she said. "I've been practicing lots."

"All right already. I'm coming." Anyways, I wasn't in any hurry to watch Sadie and Aaron make goo-goo eyes at each other all afternoon. And Lena was all excited.

"Today I'm going to make it all the way," she announced. "You watch."

"Better hurry up before it gets too crowded."

Lena jumped in and swam beside the rope between the shallow end and the deep end. Her behind wiggled like a little fish. Not exactly a smooth swimmer, but she got the job done. The lifeguard was standing close by, which gave me an idea. I went over and asked if he would watch my little sister.

See, to get into the deep end and use the diving boards, you first had to show a lifeguard that you could swim across the pool four times without stopping or anything.

Lena swam four widths no problem. When the lifeguard told her she could go in the deep end, her face lit up like a Christmas tree. First thing she wanted to do was jump off the high diving board.

The lineup was long. Half the kids in town were in the water. On a scorcher like today the pool was the only place to go.

When it was her turn, Lena walked to the end of the board and looked down. Big mistake. She just stood there like a duck on a stump, not knowing which way to turn. I

hoped she was going to be okay because the worst thing
was if a person got up there and then lost their nerve, and
had to make everyone else in line back off the ladder so
they could come down. I didn't want that to happen to
my sister.

"Go ahead." I hung onto the top of the ladder behind
her. The kids farther down were starting to make noises.
"You can do it."

And she did, too. She didn't hold her nose even like
some kids do. I watched to make sure she was all right
before I jumped, but she swam to the side, hauled herself out of the pool, and was back in line before I came
up for air.

The lineup was longer than before, all the way around
the board and along the edge of the pool, but it never made
a diff to Lena. She couldn't wipe the grin off her face.

"This time I'm going to run and jump," she said.

"Do it." I spotted my friends playing keep away – guys
against girls. Of course, every time Aaron had the ball,
Sadie was all over him. And vice versa. Even though I was
trying to forget about him and be happy for Sadie, it still
hurt to watch. So I turned away – and stepped right on
Mark Giesbrecht's foot. He was standing there behind
me, grinning like an idiot.

"What're you doing here?" I blurted. I was too surprised to hide the fact I wasn't happy to see him.

Mark's grin disappeared. He even looked a little hurt
maybe. "It's a free country, last time I looked."

Like always with Mark, I wished I had a good comeback handy. Like always, I didn't.

"Shouldn't you be out in a beet field somewhere?" I couldn't help but notice how tanned he was and how great his hair looked, all bleached by the sun.

"We finished a field this morning. It was so hot they sent us home early."

"Everyone's over there," I pointed. Hint, hint.

"I know. I want to go off the board first." Mark dipped a toe in the water. "Anyways, how come you're not playing?"

The line hadn't even reached the ladder yet. We shuffled forward slowly along the edge of the pool.

"It's my sister's first time in the deep end." I nodded at Lena, glad to have an excuse handy.

"Way to go," Mark congratulated her.

Lena grinned. "It was a cinch."

"Hey," Mark said, turning to me. "Is your mom home already from the hospital?"

Talk about out of left field. Just when I was thinking Mark maybe wasn't so bad, that *glommskopp* started talking about how his mom had gone to the hospital to visit my mom because she was on the sick list at church. Only he said his mom had come home again right away because my mom wasn't there.

"So is she in the hospital or what?"

Lena opened her mouth. She was going to tell Mark our life story right there if I didn't stop her. I poked her in the ribs with my elbow.

"What was that for?" she whined.

I hissed at her to shut up before turning to answer Mark. "Yeah," I said, "she's in the hospital."

"What's wrong with her? How come my mom couldn't find her room?"

"She's –" What was I supposed to say? She's not in the regular hospital? She's in the loony bin? "She's fine. Let's not talk about it right now."

"She's going to be okay, isn't she?"

"Didn't you hear me? I don't want to talk about it." I turned my back on him. Only Mark Giesbrecht must be missing a few leaves off his tree because he still wouldn't leave it alone.

"Hey, suit yourself. I was just asking because my mom wanted to visit and –"

"She's not in the hospital hospital," Lena butted in, totally ignoring my angry glare. "If you want to go see her, you have –"

Before she could finish talking, I shoved her in the pool. Not just a little nudge either. I body checked her a good one. It was the only thing I could think of to shut her up.

Just my luck. There were three kids doing cannonballs off the high board, one after the other – bang, bang, bang – like they do sometimes where the first one goes off to the left, the second one goes straight ahead and the third one goes off to the right. They're not supposed to do that, but they sometimes do anyways. The first kid almost landed on Lena's head. Almost.

Uy uy uy.

Mark's jaw dropped. He was too stunned to even close his mouth. A whistle blasted. The lifeguard was there already before Lena came up for air. She was okay and everything, the lifeguard could see that right away. But she made a big deal of it, making everyone in line move over by the fence and then tearing a strip off me. "Any more of that and you're out of the pool! Is that clear?"

"Yeah." I glared at Mark. I glared at Lena. Inside my chest my heart had turned into a rock or something, so hard I couldn't hardly breathe. Lena looked up at me from the water, her eyes full of hurt feelings. But I couldn't get a sorry out past the rock in my chest.

Anyways, there was nothing I could say, so I left. Lena could ride home on her own for once. Never mind Beth, that old woman – little kids roamed around town on their own all the time in Hopefield. It's not like I didn't warn Lena to keep her trap shut, or that she was made of sugar or something.

Holy Moses, what if that kid had landed on her head? My stomach flipped just thinking about it.

At first, I didn't pay much attention to where I was going. I just pedaled around. Then I found myself close to Eden. Suddenly it was like last time. I had to see Mom. I had to see her *now*. I'd been praying every day. Wasn't it high time for God to do something already?

I dropped my bike on the lawn and marched in the front door. I never stopped to think about how I looked until the nurse at the front desk did a double take. I was barefoot, my damp hair uncombed and tangled from riding. Over top of my bathing suit I had on a wrinkled T-shirt, but I wasn't wearing any shorts even.

So what? It was visiting hours. Didn't I have a right to see my own mother? I trotted by that nurse with my nose in the air.

"Wait a minute." The nurse stood up and held out her hand like a stop sign. I hurried past. By now I was shivering again, even though the place was an oven on a day like today. All I could think was, I had to see Mom. I had to let her know how everything was falling apart without her and maybe she could tell the doctors it was time for her to go home. Then she could talk to Dad about getting Tommy back and she could take care of us again instead of Beth, and I wouldn't have to look after Lena so much anymore. And maybe she'd let me have Jillian and Sadie over to make pizza or even have a pajama party for everyone. Then everything would be okay again.

My stomach went into a nosedive as I hurried down the hallway. I stopped at the door and forced myself to catch my breath or else I would've burst right into Mom's room.

She was lying in bed, all peaceful. At first I thought she was sleeping still. Her head was leaning back against her pillow, and her glasses had slid down her nose. A thin line of drool glistened at the corner of her open mouth. One hand was resting on her lap, holding a book.

I counted five heartbeats before Mom groaned and turned her head. Her eyes blinked open. They were bright. Right away my heart skipped a beat. I was thinking my real mom was maybe back, and thinking that got me so choked up I couldn't get out any words at first. I took a step toward the bed.

"*Vea es doa*?" Mom lifted her head, tilting it to one side. Her glasses fell off. She squinted a little. A tear leaked out the corner of one eye. I watched it run down her cheek as she tried to sit up. I saw the question in her teary-bright eyes just before she said, "Minnie? *Es daut du*?"

I froze. Like Lot's wife turned into a pillar of salt. Who was Minnie?

The question in Mom's eyes spilled out over her face. I watched it shudder through her whole body. Then she closed her eyes, rubbing her fingers across her forehead. The Bible on her lap slid to the floor.

"*Ach. Daut dayt me lite.*" She spoke slowly, as if the words hurt. "*Du best nich* Minnie?" She lifted her head, using her hand to wipe away the tears, and rambled on. I couldn't follow what she was saying. Only one thing I understood for sure.

Mom wouldn't be coming home. Not today. Not anytime soon.

Mom didn't know who I was even.

My skin went cold, my spine froze into an icicle. I knew I'd have to keep it that way or it would melt and there'd be nothing left to hold me up. I stumbled backwards a few steps, until I was out of the room. Then I ran.

I ran and I ran. That weird ringing filled my ears again. From far away, through the ringing, I could hear the hollow sound of bare feet slapping against the cold floor tiles. I glanced over my shoulder. No one was there.

Just my sweaty footprints evaporating as they followed me out the door.

Oh, dear God, dear God, dear God.

18

That is so long ago
It's hardly true anymore

A voice whispered warm and wet in my ear. "We don't have to go get Tommy after all."

Lena hopped on my bed and started bouncing on her knees around me. "It's morning. Stand up already, sleepy-head!"

I pulled the sheet over my head, curling up in a ball. "Go away." I didn't have the energy even to tell her to quit talking like an old Mennonite.

"But you have to get up! Dad's going to phone up Nickel Enns and get Tommy back! He said he never thought anyone would make such a big deal over an old alley cat." Lena nearly bounced on my head. "Did you really almost run away?"

Huh. So Dad figured I'd taken off because of Tommy. That was okay by me.

I never thought about where I was going after I'd run

out of Eden. I'd just jumped on my bike and started pedaling. Somehow I ended up on the highway to the States,
pedaling and pedaling and pedaling. For all I knew I
could've pedaled right across the border into North
Dakota. In the back of my mind somewhere I knew it
was too hot to be out there. I could feel myself burning,
but the burning on the outside felt good compared to the
burning in my chest and throat and eyes.

I wondered how to go about running away, but at the
same time I was wondering about it, I knew already that
I was too much of a chicken to really do it.

I don't know for sure how far I went, or if I really
would've ridden all the way to the States if Dad hadn't
happened to drive by in his half-ton. He pulled over on
the shoulder and waited for me to catch up. "Elsie!?
What in blazes are you doing out here?"

My heart kept racing after I stopped. My skin was on
fire. I tried to say something. Then my knees just bent
like rubber. Dad caught me in his arms.

"C'mon, kidlet. Let's get you home."

Dad told Beth he thought I'd maybe got too much sun.
"She needs to rest." He gave me a glass of water, made me
drink the whole thing, then tucked me into bed in my
cool, dark room. I don't remember exactly, but I think he
put a cold cloth on my forehead.

When I woke up it was dark. The cloth on my forehead was still cold yet. Someone must have changed it.
There was a glass of ice water on the night table beside

my bed. I gulped it down and right away fell asleep again.

Let Dad think what he wanted. I wasn't telling a soul what happened. So I guess there were a couple of more lies to add to my list of sins. I didn't give a care. Me and God were through.

Lena wriggled under the sheet until the tip of her nose almost touched mine. She frowned cross-eyed at me. "Elsie? Are you feeling better yet? Did you hear what I said? Dad's phoning up Nickel Enns right now!"

"I heard," I said. "That's great." I frowned cross-eyed back at her, but I couldn't make myself be as happy as she was.

"C'mon!"

Anyways, Lena was ecstatic enough for the both of us, like it never made any difference that I'd dumped her in the pool.

She giggled and whispered, "Jillian rode home with me yesterday. Mark told her to. 'Cause I told him you'd get in trouble. But now you won't!" She gave a final huge bounce, launched herself off the bed, and scooted out the door.

"Who asked them?" I muttered. I didn't care about getting in trouble. Dad shouldn't let them do whatever it was they were doing to Mom in that place. How could he just stand by and do nothing? I dragged myself downstairs, still in my pajamas.

"You're sure." Dad was frowning into the phone. He barely glanced at me shuffling into the kitchen. Then he started talking Plautdietsch, which could only mean one thing. Bad news.

Beth beat like crazy at a bowl of pancake batter. I knew already before Dad even hung up.

"*Deh kohta es ootyeklivft*," he said, forgetting at first to switch back to English until he saw our blank faces. "Tommy ran away. He disappeared the day after I dropped him off. Nickel Enns will let us know if he turns up." He kept talking, like everything was all right when it was plain as day that it wasn't. "Tommy's an alley cat. He can take care of himself."

From the way Dad never looked at us I could tell he felt pretty bad about everything. Not that he'd ever come out and actually say he was sorry. Lena crawled under the table again. She sat under there hugging her knees, scrunched up as small as she could make herself.

"That's it?" I said. "You're not going to do anything to find him?"

He threw up his hands. "What do you want me to do, Elsie? You want I should search the whole countryside for a bloody cat?"

"I don't know," I muttered, watching Dad reach for his cap. In another minute he'd walk out again.

Without thinking I blurted, "What kind of treatments are they giving Mom?"

For sure that stopped him in his tracks. I don't know who was more surprised, me or him.

"What do you mean?"

But I'd lost my nerve. My tongue was stuck to the roof of my mouth. All I could do was stand there and look at Dad's feet, wishing he would leave.

"What is it now, *meyahl?*" Dad's voice was gruff still, like always, only quieter.

Under the table Lena scooted forward on her bum to stare up at Dad and me. Beth stood perfectly still at the stove, her back toward us.

Finally my tongue loosened. "I just – I want to know what they're doing to Mom, that's all." My throat was scratchy, like there was something stuck going down the wrong way.

"You girls don't need to worry about that," Dad insisted. "She's going to be fine."

Jumping Jehoshaphat. What kind of answer was that? How could we not worry? She was our mother.

"Anyways, I already know," I rushed on. "I heard you and Auntie Nettie talking, about how Mom gets such bad headaches because of the shock treatments." Now my legs were shaking yet. I sat down on the nearest chair.

Beth put the ladle down, took the frying pan off the burner, and switched the burner off. She turned to face us, and the way she looked at me was sad and worried and kind all at once. I'd never seen her look at me like that before.

Dad ran his hand through his hair like he did all the time when he didn't know what to say. "This is why I haven't said anything. There's no good reason for you girls to get all upset over it."

"Dad." Beth was shaking her head. "We live here, remember? We're not deaf and dumb. I know about the shock treatments, too. Probably even Lena knows."

I felt a rush of gratefulness to Beth. Dad was outnumbered. Maybe now we'd finally get a real answer.

Dad sighed and pulled up a chair. "Come here *schnigglefritz*." He held his arms out to Lena. She scrambled out from under the table and crawled into his lap.

"So you girls know about the shock treatments. It's what the doctors think is best for Mom, to help her get well again."

"When is Mommy coming home?" Lena whispered.

"Soon. Another two or three weeks, maybe."

Soon was a promise cheap as borscht. "Does it mean what I think? Shock, like in electricity?"

Dad winced. "It's not so bad as it sounds."

"How can they give Mommy electricity?" Lena wanted to know.

I gagged. It was all I could do not to throw up right then and there.

"It's a special kind of medicine," Dad said to Lena. Even his voice was shaking a little, his words stumbling all over each other. "They put wires on her forehead. Doctor Shroeder says the whole thing takes less than a minute. Then after, she sleeps for awhile."

So, that meant she was awake when they did it?! *Deevilschinda.* So what if *deevilschinda* was a bad swear, it wasn't as bad as what they were doing to Mom.

"Electricity works better than pills do for some people like Mom."

"People like Mom?!" Beth slammed the frying pan back on the burner and gave the knob a hard twist. "You make it sound like she's some kind of freak."

"That's not how I meant it and you know it." Dad sounded tired. "I mean people like Mom who are depressed."

"But it gives her headaches." My voice came out barely above a whisper. How can something that gives you headaches be good for you!?

"*Nah yo,*" Dad nodded. "There are side effects. That's why she feels sore and sometimes has trouble remembering little things. But all that doesn't last too long usually. And they give pain medicine to help with the headaches."

Usually. Little things. Medicines.

They were giving my Mom shock treatments. Zapping her brain with electricity, zapping the depression right out of her.

What else was getting zapped out, I couldn't help wonder. *Zap.* There goes the depression. *Zap.* There goes a little memory along with it. Not so important. She doesn't need to know what day it is. Someone can tell her. *Zap.* Oops, there goes that memory of picking up the squished baby birds. For sure it was a bad one anyways.

Zap. Zap. Zap. Hallowe'en's gone. The piano recital, gone. Her kid's name. Gone. No problem. She'll remember her daughter tomorrow maybe. Or the next day. Or whenever.

Fuy. No wonder she slept all the time. No wonder no one wanted to tell me anything.

"The doctors know what's best for Mom," Dad insisted again. Only he said it like he was trying to convince himself. "We have to trust them."

Beth poked away at the pancakes with a spatula. "We have to pray that the treatments will work, and Mom will get well. We have to trust in God to take care of her. Just like he'll take care of Tommy, wherever he is."

Since when did Beth give a care about what happened to Tommy? And what good would praying do? I'd prayed and I'd prayed, and this was God's answer? If God didn't care enough to help Mom, why would he look out for an old stray?

God was supposed to be all powerful. The Lord God Almighty, not? If He was all powerful then He meant for all this to happen.

I couldn't imagine why. It didn't matter anyways. There wasn't a reason good enough for God to let them do things to my mother that made her forget her own kid! What greater purpose was there in that? Either God just didn't care or – He wasn't all powerful after all.

Maybe there was no God even.

This time the thought was there in my head before I could stop it. I held my breath, waiting to be struck by lightning. When I didn't incinerate or anything, I let the thought creep back. Maybe there was no God. Or if there was, maybe He wasn't the kind of God I thought He was. Maybe He wasn't the kind of God I wanted to believe in.

Still nothing happened.

"I don't believe in God," I whispered.

Only I guess I whispered louder than I thought. Dad and Beth got these terrible hurt looks on their faces like I'd slapped them or something.

"What?" said Dad.

Outside the kitchen window the sun was shining the same as always. The robins were chirping the same as always. The leaves on the trees were fluttering in the breeze still. The world hadn't changed.

But I had. I didn't feel like a kid anymore.

That is so long ago it's hardly true anymore. Mom sometimes said that to us kids, like if we were fighting about something that had happened maybe yesterday or last week.

I felt like the time when I was a kid was so long ago it was hardly true anymore, like I never even was a kid.

For sure I'd never be a kid again.

I licked my dry lips and said, as firmly as I could, "I don't believe in God anymore."

Beth sucked in her breath. Lena slid off Dad's lap and stared at me, her eyes wide. Even I couldn't quite believe what I'd said. For such a loud family, everyone was awful quiet all of a sudden.

"You don't mean that," Dad said.

"Yes, I do." Maybe I did. I didn't know. I didn't know what I believed for sure anymore.

"Elsie, don't. Don't talk like that."

"Fine then." I wasn't angry. I wasn't anything. "But I'm not going to church anymore. You can ground me if you want. Makes me no never mind."

I wasn't going to Eden anymore either, but I didn't say anything about that yet. "You can make me stay in my room forever if you want, but you can't tell me what to think. No one can tell me what I should think, or what I should believe."

It was true. Walking calmly up the stairs to my room, I knew it was true.

For once I wished I was wrong. More than anything, I wished someone would just tell me what to believe, and I'd believe it, and that would be that. Everything would be so easy if I could just believe like Beth believed or like Reverend Funk believed or like Dad, who believed after all, even if he didn't go to church all the time.

Something told me I could ride my bike around the world with no hands and the chances of my wish being granted would still be *nusht*.

19

Weddings and good haying weather

Auntie Nettie's straw hat skipped along above the gooseberry bushes almost half a row ahead already. She was singing. Not quietly to herself. She was singing out loud, in German, so everyone in the garden and the farmyard and probably out in the fields and all the way to town yet could hear her.

The firm, striped green berries fell into my pail with a satisfying plop. Picking as fast as I could, there was still no way I could keep up with Auntie Nettie. She finished her side of the row and came around the end to work her way back on my side, still singing.

Beth and Taunte Tina were stripping chokecherries into pails at the other end of the yard. Beth was on a stepladder working up high while Taunte Tina was clearing the lower branches. Taunte Tina was too big to stand on a ladder.

Two rows over, Lena was helping Grandma pick raspberries. Grandma was picking, anyways. Lena was sitting
in the dirt trying to feed one of Auntie Nettie's farm cats.
The cat's face was smeared with squished raspberry.

Grandma and Taunte Tina started singing along.

"*Und alles, alles, alles, war wieder gut.*"

I got some of the last line, something about all was
good. The old women laughed like they were little kids
and started singing the whole thing all over again. I half-
listened, the song and the sun warming me, picking gooseberries. I watched Lena play with the cat and wondered if
Tommy was all right and tried not to think too much about
Mom because when I did, I could feel the blood start to
race through my body and pound in my head.

A robin, chirping like crazy, flew practically in front of
my nose and landed on the scarecrow in the middle of the
garden. Probably it was mad that we were cleaning out all
the ripe berries.

"Don't look at me," I muttered to the robin. "I didn't
ask for this job."

Only I was sort of glad Dad made me go with to pick
berries at Auntie Nettie's this morning. It was nice being
out in the sunshine. I started leaving a few ripe berries
behind. Robins needed to eat, too, I figured. They had to
fly all the way south for the winter, not?

One of the barn cats was slinking through the garden,
its eye on the robin. Seeing it stalking that bird made me
wonder if Tommy was going hungry, or if he would

remember how to hunt still. No one was giving him shock treatments at least.

Then I stopped picking, because I was remembering something I'd read one time, about how some cats that are taken away from their homes find their way back again, even if home is miles and miles away. They're just like birds that way, they carry around a compass inside them. Sometimes.

What if Tommy had run away from the farm to go back home? To our alley. The idea wouldn't go away. I turned it over and over again in my head, and all the time I felt more and more sure that it was exactly what had happened. We didn't need to search the whole countryside at all. If Tommy was trying to get home, and if his compass was working right, he'd be somewheres between Hopefield and the farm where Nickel Enns lived. Wherever that was. North of town. I was pretty sure Dad had said something about north of town.

I could sit around waiting for Tommy to find his way home, and maybe he would and maybe he wouldn't. Maybe a coyote or a fox or an owl or a car or some farmer's tractor would get him first. Or I could get on my bike and go find him myself, before anything bad happened.

"*Nah meyahl.* Weddings and good haying weather don't come every day."

I was thinking so hard to myself I didn't notice Auntie Nettie come up. A few ripe berries tumbled from her fingers into the bucket. "We can make *kressberren mouse* enough for a thresher gang, not?"

She lifted her face to the sun. "This is the day the Lord has made. Let us rejoice and be glad in it."

Close by like this, Auntie Nettie smelled like sunshine and sweat and a bit like barn. A few stray hairs had pulled out of the bun at the back of her neck and stuck to her sweaty skin. Below her skirt, I could see the tops of her stockings rolled up and biting into her calves.

"Elsie doesn't believe in God anymore," Beth said drily. She was walking by carrying two full pails of choke-cherries into the house.

"*Fuy.*" Grandma frowned at me as she toddled past with her raspberries. "For sure you believe in God. You've believed in God all the way since you were just little."

I knew enough not to argue with Grandma.

She nodded her head toward the chokecherry bushes. "To bring the ladder to the house needs someone with a young back. Hurry yourself up."

Auntie Nettie took my half full pail of gooseberries from me and waited while I ran to fetch the stepladder.

"Is it right, what Beth says?" She was swaying beside me as I dragged the ladder to the house.

"I guess," I shrugged. I didn't really want to talk about it. Not believing in God was too new still to talk about yet. A big idea like that needed some time to try on and see how it fit.

"You guess? *Nay, meyahl*, you don't guess about God. You know him, here." She set the berry pails on the grass and put a hand over her heart. "And here." Her hand swept across the sky and the prairie. "And here." She bent down to grab a handful of black earth from the garden and held it to her nose, breathing deep before letting it sprinkle back to the ground.

"And here." Auntie Nettie wrapped both arms around me, squeezing tight for a long time. When she let go she held my shoulders and looked me in the eye. "Or you don't."

I'd never heard anyone talk like that before about God, like He was part of everything. Not up in heaven looking down watching you all the time, but just – here.

Auntie Nettie's eyes twinkled. "You are too much thinking all the time. Come eat."

In no time the kitchen table was piled with plates of farmer sausage and bowls of *varenika* swimming in *schmauntfat*. There was cole slaw and fresh garden peas with baby carrots and homemade buns to fill in the gaps. And a fresh-baked saskatoon berry pie sitting on the counter making my mouth water with how good it smelled.

"Who will say the blessing?" asked Grandma Redekop.

Everyone folded their hands and bowed their heads. Everyone except me. While Uncle Abe said grace, I stared hard at my plate. At least he said a short one.

"Come Lord Jesus be our guest, and let this food to us be blest. Amen."

Grandma must not have had her eyes closed either, because when Uncle Abe finished she wanted him to say it again. "I think not everybody was ready." She was frowning so hard at me her eyebrows almost touched in the middle, just like Lena's.

Only Uncle Abe was already spearing sausages onto his plate. "The Lord knows we're all grateful, *Mutta*."

Lena was watching Uncle Abe reach for the bowl of vegetables. He winked at her. The corners of her mouth twitched. She already knew what was coming next, same as me.

"You know," said Uncle Abe, "the cook who cooks carrots and peas in the same pot –"

"Is an unsanitary cook!" Lena shouted out the punch line, giggling. Everyone else groaned or shook their heads and ignored them.

Auntie Nettie slapped Uncle Abe on the shoulder. "All the time with that terrible joke. When will you be tired of it already?"

He pulled her toward him, wrapping both arms around her. "I'm not tired of you yet, am I?"

"*Ach, du hundt.*" Auntie Nettie squirmed out of his arms.

Usually I liked watching everyone kibitzing and having themselves a good time. Only today it didn't feel right that we could have such a good time without Mom. Not when she was having such a miserable time.

I filled my plate with *varenika* and vegetables. When the plate of farmer sausages got to me I took some of those, too. Far as I was concerned, all deals with God were off. If there was a God even.

What would Mom say when she came home and found out Tommy was gone? She'd be awful sad. Heartbroken even. What if she was so sad she ended up going back to Eden and they gave her more of those shock treatments?

I couldn't let that happen.

Dad wasn't going to do anything to get Tommy back. Beth didn't care one iota about him. Lena was still too small yet. And I sure couldn't count on God. So it was up to me. Besides which, it was mostly my fault Tommy was lost. Just like it was mostly my fault Mom was even in that place. Right now finding Tommy was the best way I could think of to make one thing right again at least.

Incredible Journey. That was the name of the book where I'd read about the cat and the two dogs finding their way home. Now I remembered. But I couldn't remember for sure if it was one of the dogs who was the leader, or if it was the cat.

Beth jabbed me in the ribs with her elbow. "What happened to being a vegetarian?" She nodded at the sausage on my plate.

It was hard to ignore the smug look on her face, but I had more important things to think about than arguing with Beth.

"I gave it up," I said. "You were right. It was dumb."

That shut her up. She wasn't expecting me to say she was right about something.

It wasn't like I was completely stupid. I knew the chances of finding Tommy were slim and none. That didn't make a diff. I had to try.

For once I wasn't going to be such a chicken. For once I wasn't going to just think about what I wanted to do, I was going do it.

When everyone was busy yakking in Plautdietsch and laughing all over themselves, I leaned toward my uncle. "Uncle Abe?" I asked. "Do you know where Nickel Enns lives?"

Anyways, like Auntie Nettie said already, weddings and good haying weather don't come every day.

20

Could we with ink the ocean fill

Dad came downstairs Sunday morning in slacks and a freshly pressed shirt yet, too. "I thought I'd go with to church. I'll even take my girls out to the Harvester for dinner after."

He didn't fool me. He was only going to church because of what I'd said about not believing in God. Like he was going to be a good example or something. As if. All my plans were about to fly out the window if Dad made me go to church.

"I told you already, I'm not going," I said.

Dad threw up his hands. "Have it your way. I'm tired of fighting with you. But if you're not going to church you're not going out to eat with us either."

"No problem." It never bothered me to get left behind. It would even be a good thing.

"Do you want some eggs or not?" Beth scowled at me as she hovered over my plate with the frying pan.

"Not. I'll have cereal." I was all out of kilter this morning. My nerves were on end waiting for everyone to leave so I could put my plan into action.

"Mom asked about you last night," Beth nattered on. "Haven't you been to see her?"

"I was there Thursday." I wasn't going back to that place. Not ever.

"You can stop by this afternoon then."

"I'm going swimming this afternoon," I lied. "Anyways, there are too many people there on Sundays." I figured when everyone got back from dinner and found out I wasn't home, they'd think I was at the pool. I had until *faspa* later this afternoon before anyone would realize I was gone. Hopefully I'd be back by then.

Beth shook her head. "You can't spare an hour to visit your own mother?"

"Go jump in a lake."

"Five minutes," said Dad, talking through clenched teeth. "Can't you two quit squabbling for five minutes?"

I shut my mouth, only because I didn't want to say anything that would keep them home a minute longer than necessary.

As soon as they left, I filled an empty plastic milk jug with water and stuffed it into my pack with a couple of sandwiches, an apple, and some cookies. What else did

I need? I put on a floppy hat, the one Mom used for gardening. Already I could tell today was going to be another scorcher.

Lastly, I rinsed out Tommy's dish and filled it with fresh milk, just in case he maybe came back on his own while I was gone.

I didn't have to worry about Grandma Redekop looking out her window. All the old folks were at church like most everyone else. It was a clean getaway.

Singing – a German hymn – leaked out of the MB church as I pedaled by. It made me feel small and alone, to be out here when everyone else was in there. Jillian might have come with if I'd asked her. I'd almost called her last night. Only she hadn't called me once since going away with Sadie.

I pedaled a bit farther past the church and left the singing behind.

Ten minutes later, I was at the highway north of town. The traffic was pretty steady here because it was the main highway to Winnipeg and Steinbach and the Pembina Hills and the States even – pretty much anywhere a person wanted to go. I had to wait a long time to cross.

Then I had to decide whether to follow the highway west for a bit, or head straight north. West would take me to the Three-mile Corner, and from there another highway went north to the Bible camp. Uncle Abe had said Nickel Enns lived north and west of town past the Bible camp. If I was right, Tommy could be wandering anywhere between here and there. I couldn't very well ride my bike cross-country, except for some places where there were farmer roads between the fields. But I could follow the gravel section roads, up one mile, one mile over, up a mile, over a mile, until either I found Tommy or else it was time to head home.

Who knows? Maybe I'd get lucky, I kept telling myself. Only even while I was telling myself, my heart was sliding into my running shoes. I knew this whole idea was pretty lame, but I didn't give a care. Besides which, I didn't have any other ideas, good or bad.

I decided to head north on the gravel road, because there wasn't much traffic, and anyways, Tommy wasn't going to follow the highways.

Almost right away trouble caught up to me. I'd hardly got started, when I heard someone shouting my name. I looked behind me and nearly wiped out.

There was Lena, pedaling like crazy toward the highway, waving and yelling at me. "Elsie! Wait up once!"

Holy Moses. I turned around and raced back, shouting, "Stay there!"

Of course the *dummkopp* never listened.

"I want to go with!" She started across the highway, not stopping even to check if there was any traffic. Like the semi headed toward town at full speed was invisible.

"LOOK OUT!" I screamed. My heart practically leaped across the road to tackle her. The semi's horn blasted. Lena plowed on the brakes and the semi roared by, belting me with hot wind and bits of gravel that stung my bare arms and legs. I turned my head, closing my eyes.

Then the truck was gone, and when I looked again there was Lena standing on the other side, still in one piece even if she had gone white as a sheet. Holy Moses.

If I didn't do something quick my little sister was going to get smucked like a gopher. "Don't move until I tell you!" I yelled across the road. Soon there was a break in traffic and then Lena was safe and sound beside me.

Now what was I supposed to do? Either I dragged her along or I had to give up before I even got started. So it goes always.

You bet she knew it, too. "I'll go by myself if you don't let me come with. I want to look for Tommy too."

"How did you know I was going to look for Tommy?"

"I'm not stupid. You were wearing running shoes this morning." Lena's eyes flashed with triumph. "You never wear shoes in summer if you don't have to."

We both looked at the clunky high-tops on Lena's feet. She was wearing my beat-up old runners instead of the white buckle sandals she usually wore to church with her little blue sundress. *Uy uy uy.*

"My runners are too small," she said.

That little *baydel* had only pretended to go to Sunday School. Instead she'd snuck through the church basement and out the back door that we use for choir practice. Then she ran home and followed me. She had more guts than I did, that was for sure. Only thing was, now

Dad and Beth would know something was up right away when Sunday School was over already.

I tried not to think about how much trouble we were going to be in when we got home.

"It's your funeral if you get sunburned." I took off my hat and plopped it on her head. "You wear that, and you do what I tell you. Got it?"

"Got it," she grinned.

❧

The going was slower than I'd thought it would be. Partly because of Lena, but also partly because it was hard to pedal through the loose gravel. Even when we tried to stick to the hard-packed places we still had to ride close enough to the ditch to check if there was any sign of Tommy.

Every once in a while someone would drive by, and then I'd herd Lena over to the side of the road until the clouds of dust kicked up by the car or truck settled down again. At least the day wasn't scorching, not yet anyways. It was sunny, but there were a few clouds to cool things off once in a while. As long as we kept pedaling the breeze felt cool.

Except for when a car passed, it was kind of nice being out there on the country roads. The fields of grain and rapeseed smelled good – earthy and sun ripe and just a bit sweet mixed all up with the perfume of fresh cut alfalfa and wildflowers growing in the ditches.

Meadowlarks sitting on fence posts sang out all happy and bright. Every so often Lena would call out Tommy's name. But except for Lena and the birds, pretty much the only sounds were the crunch of our bike tires on the road and the click-whir of grasshoppers jumping out of our way.

One time we rode up the crest of a hill and we both stopped. Flowing out from the sides of the road ahead was a blue, blue ocean of flax. The breeze made the flax move like waves, lapping at the road. Riding between the fields felt almost like we were with Moses, walking through the Red Sea, on our way to the promised land.

We turned west at the first section road, and then north again at the next.

"Lookit," Lena pointed. A little ways ahead a hawk was hovering over the summer fallow. All of a sudden it dropped to the ground, feet first. It lifted off again with a mouse in its claws.

Then we pedaled past a porcupine waddling along the side of the road. When we got too close it disappeared, slipping into the tall grass in the ditch. I knew it was there but I couldn't see it. Spotting Tommy in that grass was pretty much hopeless. The only reason I kept going was pure stubbornness. I wasn't going to give up, at least not without trying. We had to find Tommy, that's all there was to it. I couldn't stand to think of the look on Mom's face if she came home and he wasn't there.

And then I heard a truck coming up behind, so I told

Lena to move over to the side again. The truck was going pretty slow when it passed, and crowding so close that we both hit the ditch. Even after it went by and we pushed our bikes back on the road again the truck was driving still slower yet, staying a little ways ahead of us.

That truck gave me the creeps. It looked familiar but I couldn't think why. "Let's stop for a minute," I said.

"I'm thirsty." Lena licked her dry lips. Even with Mom's hat on, her face was getting red.

I dug out my water, all the time watching the truck. But then it sped up again when another car passed, so that was all right, and it was just my imagination running away on me.

Lena was guzzling so much water I had to snatch it away from her. I swallowed a few mouthfuls. The jug was half empty already. But I wasn't too worried. We could stop at a farmhouse and fill it up again.

"Did you bring something to eat, too?" Lena said hopefully.

"What do you think? We'll find a shady spot and have lunch." I could see Lena was starting to get sunburned on her arms already. My nose was probably red as a beet. That *gurknaze* was always the first thing to get burned. We needed to get out of the sun for a while. Probably we'd have to head back home after that.

We turned west again at the next crossroads. It was almost noon I guessed, and plenty hot enough now. The sun was burning my arms and the back of my neck. We'd seen a couple of cats already, but no sign of Tommy. Up ahead I could see some bush, which meant there was maybe a creek, too. I was thinking that might be a good spot to rest a bit.

To get to the bush we first had to ride by a row of big trees in front of a farmyard. Just when we were almost by already, a huge dog came darting out of the trees, barking its fool head off.

"ELSIEEE?!" Lena shrieked. Like I was supposed to know what to do.

"Get going! Quick! It'll stop at the end of the yard." At least that's what I was hoping for. We were pedaling like crazy, trying to outrace that dog. Ahead of me Lena was still shrieking, and behind me the dog was running alongside, barking at my heels. Past the farmyard we rode over a small rise and then we were going still faster yet, pedaling downhill. The dog slowed down a bit so we were gaining ground at least.

Then Lena's front wheel hit a patch of loose gravel, and just like that, down she went. Total wipe out, right into the ditch.

She lay there, screaming like all get out. I skidded to a stop in the gravel and ran over, thinking it was a good thing that she was crying. At least she wasn't knocked out or anything. But her bike was lying on top of her and before I could haul it off I had to untangle her foot from between the bars. She didn't bawl any harder and she could sit up all right and move everything, so I was pretty sure nothing was broken. But she had a doozy of a scrape up one side of her leg. Her elbow and shoulder were smucked up pretty bad, too, and her sundress was filthy, with a long rip in the skirt.

Good thing she'd fallen into the ditch and not onto the road. Someone had a guardian angel close by.

I used the rest of our water to wet the bottom of my T-shirt and clean her off as good as I could. Soon she started to calm down. Her crying turned into hiccups and sniffles.

"I want – *hic* – to go home."

All the time I was cleaning her up I was keeping one eye on the dog. It was sitting there at the end of the row of trees, watching. But I guess that dog was happy enough with having chased us past its yard. Still, I didn't really want to go back that way. I was starting to figure out that this whole thing wasn't just lame, it was stupid. As if there was any real chance of finding Tommy out here. It figured that Dad would be right. And now Lena was hurt. It was time to call it quits before anything else went wrong.

"Yeah, okay," I said. "See if you can stand up."

She could stand on her own two feet all right, even if she was a bit wobbly and winced when she stepped on her one foot. I made her walk it off by the side of the road. I was brushing the dirt off her clothes when a pick-up pulled close beside us and stopped. A man rolled down the window. "You kids need some help?"

"We're all right, thanks," I glanced quickly at him, but he wasn't someone I knew. So I looked away again and hoped he would leave.

"Sure you don't need a ride somewhere? The little girl looks hurt."

I didn't like how he sounded too much. Or how he looked sort of sideways toward the farmyard behind us. And there was something weird about his beat-up brown truck with the white shell over the back. The knot in my gut tightened.

Lena was pulling on my sleeve. "Let's get a ride home, Elsie."

"Shhh!" I whispered, leaning close and pretending to fix her hair up. "We don't take rides from strangers, remember?"

Lena's eyes opened wide. She nodded.

"No, thanks," I told him. Then I pointed to the next farm up ahead a ways and out-and-out lied. "We just live there."

The man glanced at the farm. He shrugged. "If you say so."

He closed his window and the truck pulled away, slowly. Instead of driving off the truck was crawling along ahead, like the guy was watching and waiting to see what we would do next.

And then I knew what it was that was bothering me about that truck. It was the same one that had run us into the ditch before. I was pretty sure it was the same one I'd seen on the street and by the pool, too, except now the back of the truck had been covered.

My imagination took off at a gallop.

"C'mon, you have to get on your bike," I told Lena.

"My leg hurts."

The dog was sitting there at the corner of its yard still. It had stood up but stayed put when the truck stopped. If that dog hadn't been there, I would've turned Lena around and pedaled straight back to that farmhouse right then.

"I know." I picked up her bike. "Only you have to get on the bike and ride anyways. Just to the next farm. Can you make it that far? I don't want to stay on the road with that man watching us."

Lena straddled her bike. "Is he a bad man?"

"I don't know. He might be."

We pedaled slowly, but the truck stayed in sight up ahead the whole time. I was hoping that the lie I told about where we lived had long enough legs to get us home safe and sound. When we finally reached the next driveway, I breathed a huge sigh of relief.

Lena looked around nervously. "What if there's another dog?"

"Then we pretend that it's ours," I said, sounding braver than I felt. "Let's just hope someone is home."

For once we had a bit of luck. We followed the driveway along a row of evergreens and no dog came bounding after us.

"In here." The driveway turned into the yard behind a tangled clump of lilacs and caragana. Lena stayed with our bikes out of sight of the road while I went up to the house.

That was when I figured out how come everything was so quiet, when I saw the rickety old house with no paint left on it even. And how come the bushes were all overgrown. The farm was abandoned. I tried the door, just in case. It wouldn't budge.

"He's still there," Lena called. "I can see the truck through the trees."

Sure enough, the half-ton was parked a little ways up the road. Maybe there was a good reason for it to be stopped there, but I didn't like it much. What if that guy already knew nobody lived at this place?

"I want to go home," Lena repeated. "Phone up Dad and tell him to come get us."

"This place is deserted. There is no phone."

"Elsie! He's coming back!"

She was right. The half-ton swung around right there in the middle of the road and was heading our way.

"C'mon!" Grabbing our bikes, we raced across the farmyard and behind the sagging barn. I was trying to think what we should do, and what that guy might do if he found us, and at the same time I was looking for a place to hide. We could hide in the barn, only that was probably the first place he'd look.

Then I saw a road, more like two dirt ruts really, leading through the pasture behind the barn. The road ran beside the fence separating the pasture from a field. At the other end of the pasture, maybe half a mile away, was some bush. The guy might give up rather than look in the woods. At least there'd be places to hide.

"This way." The loop of wire that held the gate shut was tight, too tight for me to pull it off. My fingers slipped and I sliced myself a good one on a sharp end poking out.

"Hurrryyy!" Lena looked over her shoulder.

We shoved our bikes under the bottom wire and crawled through after. In two seconds we were racing like mad down the dirt track, scattering a flock of pigeons having lunch in the field. Looking back, my heart sank. If the pigeons hadn't given us away already, we were in clear sight of anyone who came out behind the barn. And our bikes were kicking up a trail of dust a blind man could follow. Never mind that Lena was falling behind. She was crying, and I knew her sore foot was making it hard for her to pedal.

We were never going to make it all the way to the woods. I thought about maybe hiding in the field, only the grain didn't look tall enough.

Then I saw this huge old tree, standing all by itself a short way off the track. I had another bright idea, and steered Lena toward the tree, bouncing over the rough pasture. We ducked behind it, peeking out to see if the man was following still.

He was out of his truck, standing at the gate behind the barn. I couldn't see too well from here, but it looked like he was trying to unhook the wire. One thing for sure, he wasn't trying to be a good Samaritan. My imagination wasn't running hog wild for no reason.

"What are we going to do?" whispered Lena, sniffling a little but trying hard to stop crying.

Good question. I put my arm around her and hugged her close. She was shaking, but then so was I. All I could think was that we were done for, because you bet he'd seen us. No way could we outrun him to the woods, not with Lena's sore ankle and with him in a truck. About all we could do was climb the tree. It was a big one, and we should be able to get pretty high up. Maybe he wouldn't climb up after us.

Yelling for help wouldn't do any good. There wasn't a soul around to hear us.

A loud snort startled us. Something really big gave a still louder snort behind us.

"What was that?" Lena's eyes were huge.

There was another really, really loud snort. *Uy uy uy*.

"Don't move," I whispered. Slowly, I peered over my shoulder. A bull stood there close by, too close. A huge bull. It paced back and forth, stopping to snort and paw the ground with one hoof, swinging its head low.

"Lena," I said, as calmly as I could while my insides

were shaking all over the place. "I'm going to boost you up this tree, okay? Climb up as fast as you can."

For the second time, that tree turned out to be handy. Lena scrambled up onto the lowest branch with a little help from me. I shimmied up right behind her, not a minute too soon, either. My feet were barely off the ground when the bull charged straight at us. Lena let loose, screaming her head off.

Holy Moses. I yanked my feet up, closed my eyes and hung on, waiting to be pierced through. At least this was probably a better ending than if that man in the truck had got to us first.

Only nothing happened, except I heard the loudest snort yet and practically felt that bull's hot smelly breath. The hairs on the back of my neck stood on end, that's for sure. But the bull must have veered off at the last second, because when I got up the guts to look, it was circling around and getting ready to come at us again.

"Go, go!" I shoved my little sister higher up the tree.

One good thing. From up here we had a pretty good view of the pasture and the farmyard, too. As soon as I was sure we were out of the bull's reach, I looked to see if that man was still there. He was. He was sitting in his truck, watching the fun. Maybe he couldn't unlatch the gate, either. Or maybe he didn't want to tangle with the bull.

Anyways, we weren't going anywhere, not with a bull pawing around the tree and that creep hanging around the gate. Another good thing. The man couldn't get to us either, not as long as that bull stuck close. As scared as I was of the bull, I was awful glad we'd run into him because I was still more scared of the man. I never would have thought I'd be so happy to be chased up a tree by a bull.

And that's pretty much how we stayed, for I don't know how long. Hours. If there was a God, he was a real practical joker.

One time, the man climbed through the fence and came walking toward us, until he wasn't much more than a stone's throw away. He started whooping and hollering at that bull, trying to scare him off. Only I guess the bull didn't scare too easy and didn't much appreciate more uninvited company in his pasture because he took off after the guy. The man scrambled back over the fence just barely in time to keep from being turned into a shish kebab.

For hours that ornery old bull would trot off a little ways, then come charging back to see if we were still there. Then he'd trot off again toward the truck and just stand there, keeping an eye on things, pawing the ground and shaking its head every once in a while, to make sure we knew who was the boss of this pasture. It was pretty scary, when he charged at the tree. But then if he got too far away, Lena and I hollered and hooted until he came back to see what all the commotion was about. Because that man in the truck was staying put, and I knew as soon as the bull disappeared he'd be coming after us.

We ate our lunch up in the tree. At least we ate the sandwiches. I thought we should save the apple and cookies because who knew how long we'd be stuck up here? But the bull all of a sudden got bored and started to trot away, and even when we hollered, he didn't come back. I grabbed my pack and swung it around and threw it as hard as I could. I forgot the apple and cookies were still inside it. At least the bull trotted over to investigate. He nosed around, pawing at the pack with his hoof. By the time he was satisfied, he had done a pretty good job of trampling my pack into the dirt. But he stuck close after that, maybe waiting to see what else was going to fall out of that tree, or maybe just enjoying the only bit of shade in the pasture. Whatever the reason, it was worth losing the apple and cookies.

Lena was starting to look not so good. She was awfully pale. The tree at least gave us some shade from the sun. That guy in his truck must be burning up. I hoped he was. I hoped between the bull and the sun he'd have to give up soon.

"We could sing," I suggested. Singing might even drive the man away. Beth was always saying how neither one of us could carry a tune. Hopefully the bull wouldn't mind.

Anyways, we had to do something to keep from thinking about being scared. So we sang. First we sang songs from *Mary Poppins* and *My Fair Lady* and *The Sound of Music*. Then we sang all the camp songs we knew: "Row Row Row Your Boat," "Land of the Silver Birch," "This Land is Our Land." We sang songs from church choir:

"Joy is like the Rain," "Dominique." We sang Christmas songs: "Away in the Manger," "O Tannenbaum," "Silent Night."

We sang "Jesus Loves the Little Children" and "He's Got the Whole World in His Hands" about a hundred times. First we sang all the regular verses, and then we sang a bunch of made-up verses like "He's got little sister Lena in his hands," and "He's got that big old bull, in his hands."

In between singing we tried to remember all the books of the Old Testament and we recited Bible verses. To keep Lena's mind off things, I said we should have a contest to see who knew more. I'd already had years of looking up Bible verses during sword drill at school, so I knew I could beat her pretty easy, but in the end I let her win by pretending I didn't know John 3:16. As if. And then I taught her to recite the poem "Abou Ben Adhem," which Mom had taught me in grade 3 already, but I knew it still. I wondered how Mom was doing, whether she was as scared as we were. So scared my skin was gooseflesh all over inside and outside never mind how hot it was.

"Do you think God is watching out for us right now?" Lena asked. "Do you think He'll send someone to chase the bad man away and get that old bull out of here so we can climb down?"

"Maybe." I thought about praying, just in case there really was a God. It couldn't hurt. Unless there really was a God and He was maybe mad at me for not believing in

Him until things got bad. It didn't seem right to turn to God only when there was nothing else left to turn to. If I was God, I wouldn't like being a last resort.

I was getting awful tired and uncomfortable. Even sheltered in a tree, the heat was starting to get to me. The hotter it got, the more bugs and bees there were checking us out. We had no food and no water. And Lena's eyes were starting to close. If we went to sleep up here we'd fall for sure.

"Let's sing some more." I tried to perk up and sound cheerful.

"I don't know any more songs," Lena whined.

"Sure you do." But the only songs I could think of that we hadn't sung yet were hymns. I sang quietly, because I didn't have much voice left.

"*The love of God is greater far than tongue or pen, could ever tell. It goes beyond the highest star and reaches to the lowest hell.*"

It used to be one of my favorite hymns, when I went to church still. Lena joined in on the chorus.

"*The love of God, so rich and pure, so measureless and strong. It shall forever more endure, the saints' and angels' song.*"

Usually the songs we sang in church gave me a nice warm feeling inside, especially this song. I didn't think I would feel like that today. I was too tired and too sore and too scared, and I was stuck up a tree after all. But singing was the only way I knew to keep from being still more scared yet.

"Could we with ink the ocean fill, and were the skies of parchment made, were ev'ry stalk on earth a quill, and ev'ry man a scribe by trade; to write the love of God above would drain the ocean dry; Nor could the scroll contain the whole, tho' stretched from sky to sky."

I leaned back against the tree trunk and peered up at the huge blue sky that stretched as far as I could see in every direction. Puffy, white cottonball clouds floated across it. The fields of grain on the other side of the rolling pasture shone all golden in the sun.

All around us everything was so beautiful. Even stuck up in a tree with a mean old bull waiting to rip our guts out, and some creep hanging around hoping to get his hands on us, the world still looked beautiful.

The Lord is my Shepherd, I shall not want. The familiar psalm ran through my head. *He maketh me to lie down in green pastures: He leadeth me beside still waters. He restoreth my soul.*

Well, we weren't exactly lying down, but for sure we were in a green pasture.

The thing was, I did feel better. Calmer. Lena felt better, too, I could tell. Hurt as she was, she sat beside me, swinging her legs, singing, and smiling.

For a little while, I forgot to be frightened and tired.

And then I heard the truck engine start up.

"Look!" squealed Lena. "He's leaving!"

Sure enough. The truck turned and drove away. We watched it circle around the barn and could hear it still as it gunned across the farmyard, and after a bit, we even saw a cloud of dust off in the direction of the gravel road.

"Holy Moses. He gave up," I whispered. "He got fed up with waiting."

The relief was so huge we couldn't help it. Lena and I hugged each other and cried. Then we started singing again, only this time we weren't singing because we were scared, but only because we were so happy.

Our singing was pretty bad, I guess. We'd never make it to *Hymn Sing*, anyways. But it wasn't so bad as to scare off the bull. He stayed right there under the tree, every so often wandering over to push at my pack with his nose. Until one time when he tossed it around, one of the straps caught on his horn. When the bull shook his head, the pack twirled around and landed on the back of his neck. That set him off. He snorted, shook his head again, stomped, and charged around and around the tree in circles.

We nearly laughed ourselves to death, sitting there stuck up a tree, singing our hearts out.

∿

Thunderclouds began to build later that afternoon. Maybe it was evening already, for all I knew.

High in a tree in the middle of a pasture wasn't the smartest place to wait out a thunderstorm, but it looked like that's exactly what we'd be doing. We were going to get soaked yet on top of everything. I held on to Lena and we watched the storm come closer while we kept getting more and more tired and stiff and hungry.

Thunder started to grumble. At first it was off in the distance, but it got closer all the time. Clouds started to billow higher and higher, as if they were climbing over each other to see how high they could get. It was kind of neat, watching that, seeing the storm growing.

Probably the bull didn't like the look of what was coming either, because just like that, he finally gave up and trotted off out of sight. My pack was still swinging from one of his horns.

Before we left the shelter of the tree, we took a good look around for any sign that the guy had come back. The coast was clear. Scrambling down from the tree took a whole lot longer than scrambling up had. For sure we were too stiff and sore to set any speed records, but we pedaled back to the farmyard as fast as we could in case that bull decided to come back after all. By the time we reached the barn, the sky was dark and the first big fat rain drops were beginning to splash into the dirt. Suddenly the sky lit up, and this huge crack of thunder, almost on top of us, made our hair stand on end.

We needed to find shelter quick. The house seemed like a better place to wait out the storm than the barn, where who knew what kind of animals were living. So I picked up a good-sized rock and threw it as hard as I could through a window. I felt a bit guilty, but not so guilty to keep me from doing it. Once I knocked out the glass with a stick, I crawled through and got the door open for Lena. Just in time, too.

It was all of a sudden like the sky opened and the water just came gushing out.

Flash after flash of lightning lit up the sky. Thunder rumbled through the house with hardly any break. At first it was scary, but pretty soon we got used to it.

For a long time we stood at the open doorway, watching the storm settle in around us. One thing for sure, we weren't going anywhere until it let up.

I was so tired I couldn't think. I knew we needed to get to a house and use a phone. We needed a hot bath and something to eat. We needed a soft bed. Any bed. We needed Mom and Dad and Beth, too.

Only all we had was each other. And a place to get in out of the rain, even if it wasn't much to look at. A thick layer of dust covered everything and kept making us sneeze. In some places the floor was rotting so we had to be careful where we stepped. Water dripped from the ceiling.

"I don't want to stay here." Lena whimpered softly.

She'd been so brave. I never knew how brave my little sister was before. For sure she was no dishrag.

"We're having an adventure, that's all. Just like in a story." Only in stories the kids always seemed to have everything they needed with them, or else they found what they needed right around the corner. In the adventure stories from the library, Jack and Lucy and Philip and

Dinah always had rugs and ginger beer and torches and food, no matter what kind of scrape they got themselves into.

"I'm sorry I got you into this mess," I said. "And I'm sorry about shoving you into the pool the other day."

"That's okay," she said.

We found a corner without any drips and huddled together. Lena snuggled against me. Lucky for us it was the middle of the summer, so it wasn't really cold or anything.

"I want to go home," she said softly.

"Me, too. Soon as the storm lets up."

"What if that man comes back?"

"He won't. Not in this storm." Just in case I got up and shoved an old chair under the doorknob.

"Do you think Dad is looking for us?"

"Sure he is. When the rain stops we'll phone him up and he'll come get us." I figured Dad would have started to worry when Lena didn't show up for church. He'd probably have checked with the Sunday School teachers right away after the service. When he saw our bikes were gone he'd probably have called Jillian's to ask if she knew where we were. Maybe he'd have driven down to the pool, or even checked if we had gone to see Mom at Eden.

But when we never showed up for *faspa*, then he'd probably called the police. They'd be out looking for us already. Only problem was, no one would know where to look. Everyone would be frantic. I'd stirred up a whole lot of *mouse* this time, that's for sure.

"Where will Tommy go in the rain?" Lena muttered, already half-asleep.

Tommy. I'd almost forgotten the reason we were out here, it seemed like so long ago since we'd left on our search. "He'll find a dry spot to hide, like under a log or something. Tommy's a pretty smart cat. He's managed to stay alive this long all on his own, hasn't he?" Here I was, starting to sound like Dad yet.

Something scritched in the wall behind us. Mice. I shuddered, but was too wiped out to give a care. As long as it wasn't rats.

Lightning flashed through the house, making all kinds of creepy shadows rush toward us. *I'll just close my eyes for a little while*, I thought.

❧

Dear God, I started praying. I was too tired to think of what to pray for, so I just said the prayer I used to say all the time when I was little even though it always sort of scared me because I didn't want to die in my sleep, and anyways, what if God thought I was dead when I was really only sleeping and came and took my soul away.

Now I lay me down to sleep, I pray the Lord my soul to keep. If I should die before I wake, I pray the Lord my soul to take. Amen.

I didn't remember that I didn't believe in God anymore until I was finished praying already.

21

Holy Moses

The dark was so dark I couldn't see my hand in front of my face. Beside me, I could hear Lena's soft, even breathing, and close by, the slow steady drip, drip, drip of the leaky roof.

Until a few seconds ago I'd been sleeping, too. I was wide awake now, though, listening to Lena breathe – and something else, too. Something else had woken me up. My heart jumped. The panic sat there, a lump in my throat that wouldn't go back down. I froze, listening.

Was someone trying to get in? For a long time I couldn't move.

Finally, I inched up the wall until I was standing and groped my way to the door. All the time I held my breath, listening to the silence. There was no sound of a truck engine or footsteps or rain or – anything. It was almost too silent.

Slowly, carefully, I moved the chair, opening the door just enough to peer outside. I still couldn't see or hear a thing. So I pushed the door wider, holding my breath, waiting. Waiting to hear what it was that had woken me up. After a long time surrounded by silence, I worked up the nerve to step outside.

Then I knew how come I couldn't see anything, why the world seemed so silent.

Ghosts drifted by. Fog ghosts curled around the farmyard. Ghosts with yawning grins that swallowed trees and bushes whole, then spit them right back out again. Ghosts that circled fences, ghosts that slithered up hydro poles, and hollow-eyed ghosts that peered into windows. Ghosts that swirled around outbuildings, slid between the cracks of loose boards, and crept in and out of the barn. Bits of the farmyard disappeared, then reappeared. Now you see it, now you don't. I'd catch sight of a bush or a fence post, then it would vanish and something else would appear out of the mist.

After a while I thought I noticed a rhythm in the way things appeared and disappeared, in the way the ghosts moved. It was like they were dancing. The rhythm of their dance was the same as my heart thumping in my chest. If I stayed perfectly still, I could almost hear the music, somewhere deep inside me.

All is calm. The familiar words were there in my head. Anyways, Lena and I had just been singing them when we were stuck up the tree.

The air smelled like night and rain, like wet grass and trees, earth and honeysuckle. Like silent ghosts. Sweet and fresh after the stuffy, dusty, micey smell inside the house.

No moon shone. No yard lights or house lights or streetlights. There was only the night and the dancing ghosts. And me.

Something told me to close my eyes. Right away I did, never stopping to wonder why I'd want to do that. I put my head back, tasting the mist on my lips, feeling it brush my face, then tickle my spine with light, shivery fingers.

Then – I felt something change, like a pause in the music. So I opened my eyes again. And all my breath just went out of me.

Holy Moses. Holy Moses.

The mist had parted. It was hugging the ground now. And above me the sky exploded with stars.

There in the heavens were stars of every kind you could imagine – sparkling diamonds, flickering fire-flies, and tiny pinprick stars yet, too. I walked out into the middle of the farmyard. Everywhere I turned there were stars.

Silent night, holy night. All is calm, all is bright.

The sky flowed over. Stars spilled from the Milky Way. There was hardly sky enough to hold all those stars. They were too brilliant almost to bear.

They were so brilliant, it hurt to look at them. It hurt to breathe. I thought my heart might burst.

Glory streams from heaven afar.

The fog and the stars were alive. The night was alive. Pulsing. Everything was alive and part of everything else and the crazy thing was that I was part of it, too. It was all too huge for words.

If I believed in God still, I'd think maybe this was the sign I'd prayed for. I'd think maybe I was having a vision. A glimpse of heaven.

I was standing there all alone in the night, only I wasn't so alone anymore. I felt peaceful. An ache I didn't know I had even was gone, and for the first time I could remember, I felt right. I felt whole.

Was this God then? Was this huge feeling inside me God?

I wished Mom could be here right now. I wished she could see this.

A person couldn't be sick in their heart and soul like Mom was, not if she saw something like this, something that connected you up to the whole universe.

Soon the mists closed up again. I stood there for a long time, trying to burn the feeling into my memory. Already it was slipping away. Like such terrible glory wasn't something a person could hold on to. A glimpse was all you got.

The music inside me had ended, though I didn't know when it had stopped. I was trembling. The ghosts slipped past again, still silent. I went back inside to wait out the night.

I wasn't even a bit scared anymore. Lena and I were

safe here in this farmhouse, under the stars. And now I knew what I could do to make things right with Mom. I had the beginnings of an idea. A truly brilliant idea.

First thing, Lena and I had to get home again.

Sleep in heavenly peace.

~

God was crying. His tears fell from the sky. Some of them stayed in the sky and became glistening stars. God's tears splashing on my face woke me up. I was lying on the hard, filthy floor. Water dripped from the ceiling and splashed off my face into a puddle.

Now God was in my dreams yet. Ever since I decided not to believe in Him anymore, I couldn't get Him out of my head. So it goes always.

Lena sprawled across me. I shoved her off, carefully, so I wouldn't hurt all her scrapes and bruises, and rolled over onto one elbow. I was thinking we could maybe get back to that farm with the dog and phone Dad.

Lena yawned and stretched. "Ow." She rubbed her shoulder. "I hurt. And I'm hungry." Her stomach growled, just in case I hadn't heard her.

"C'mon." I pulled her to her feet. She only limped a little bit. "Let's get out of here."

The sky was rain-washed blue, the sun already peeking up over the trees. I stood in the same place as last night. In the bright sunshine it was hard to imagine the ghosts and the countless stars. It couldn't have been a dream though, could it? I felt different. Not exactly surer. Maybe a little braver.

"I'm starving," Lena whined. "And thirsty."

We found some ripe berries in the overgrown garden behind the house, enough to keep our stomachs from grumbling too loud. There was an old well, but the pump was so rusted the handle wouldn't budge.

I could tell from the way Lena was shivering and hugging herself that she'd had about enough of this adventure. I was thinking I needed to not make too much fuss over her or else she'd fall apart yet, and then where would we be. "Never mind the stupid pump," I said. "We'll be home soon."

For all I knew, that guy in the truck drove by this place all the time. The sooner we left, the better. So we wiped our hands on the wet grass and cleaned ourselves up as good as we could. Then we hobbled down the road, pushing our bikes at first because the driveway was muddy, and anyways, we needed to work some of the stiffness out from our legs.

At least no cars or trucks passed us on the gravel road. When we reached the farm with the dog, we got off and pushed our bikes down the driveway again, all the time waiting for the hound from hell to come bounding out of the trees and chase us off. We were already halfway to the house and there was no turning back, when sure enough, the dog came trotting out of the barn.

It took one look at us and charged, barking worse than the first time. Out of the corner of my eye I saw someone follow the dog out of the barn, but I was too busy watching those teeth barreling at us to take much notice.

Lena ducked between me and her bike. We froze. The dog barked and danced all around us, sniffing and wagging his tail, then backing off and barking some more yet.

"Good dog," I murmured, trying not to sound petrified.

Woof. The dog leaped up, landing so hard with both feet on my chest that he knocked me right over. Lena screamed. I lay there flat on the ground with my bike on top of me and the dog standing over me, sniffing like I was a new kind of delicacy. This was some way to go after everything we'd been through.

"Don't worry," someone yelled. "He just wants to play with you."

Yeah, right. That's what people always said when their dogs barked and jumped up on you. "Call him off!"

"Laddie, come!"

The dog gave a last *woof*, and backed off as its owner came running up. I lay there in the dirt, panting for breath, checking to make sure if I was all in one piece still.

"*Hallemoss!* Elsie?!"

I lifted my head to look. Holy Moses was right. There stood Mark Giesbrecht, holding his dog and grinning at me.

Of all the driveways to pick from, I had to walk up his.

22

Water in the cellar pants

The best thing about painting is that a person can paint and think at the same time.

After all the kafuffle when we turned up safe and sound, I was awful glad to get a paintbrush in my hand the next day. I had a lot to think about. Everyone had made such a big deal over us, hugging and crying and thanking God and whatnot. You'd think they'd given us up for dead already after only one night missing. We were like Tom Sawyer showing up at his own funeral or something.

The wet paint glistened as I brushed it on, back and forth. Back and forth. Pretty soon the thoughts spinning around in my head slowed down enough to sort out a bit.

There were Tommy thoughts, which were sad thoughts. After everything we'd been through, our search had come to *nusht*. I might as well face it. Tommy had disappeared a week ago already. The fresh milk I'd put out last night hadn't been touched. Probably we'd never see him again. Probably Lena and I should make some kind of funeral for him.

Other thoughts in my head were about Jillian and Sadie. Jillian had phoned me up yesterday, while I was sleeping still. Once we finally got home, Lena and I had slept pretty much all day.

But Beth, she took the message for me. "I told her you and Lena were fine. She said for you to call her back."

Beth opened her mouth like she had something else to say yet, only then she didn't. She hadn't been on my case once since we got home.

It took till this morning for me to work up the nerve to phone Jillian back.

"You have some 'splaining to do, Lucy," she joked.

Right away I knew we would be all right. Only there was way too much to explain on the phone. I didn't know where to start even. So I wasn't exactly sorry Dad was making us stay home and take it easy today.

"Oh," said Jillian, when I told her.

"But will you come pick me up to go swimming tomorrow?" I blurted. "I'm not allowed to leave the house unless I'm with someone, like my parents or Beth or my friends. I'll tell you all about it then." Hopefully I wouldn't have to have a babysitter everywhere I went for the rest of the summer, but for now I figured it was a small price to pay.

"For sure!" Jillian actually sounded happy to be asked. "But you have to tell me everything."

"Everything," I promised.

"Els," she added.

"Yeah?"

"I would have gone with you, you know."

Uy uy uy. I knew I had to still come out with it and tell Jillian and Sadie I was sorry. I was pretty sure I could do it now. All I knew for sure was I wanted my two best friends back. I wanted things to be halfway normal again.

Even though I seriously doubted life would get back to normal that easily.

For one thing, that *baydel* Mark Giesbrecht was being almost nice. A whole bunch of the thoughts whirling around in my head were about him. When he'd seen who it was lying in the dirt in his farmyard, he'd laughed right out loud.

"Elsie?! Is that really you?!"

If I'd had bristles like a porcupine, they would have been standing on end right then. So what if Lena and I were covered in dirt and mice turds and cobwebs? Maybe even a little blood, too. So what if our hair looked like we'd slept in a haystack and we stunk to high heaven. I was sick of Mark making fun of me all the time. I jumped to my feet, ready to go at it.

"What are you laughing for!?" For once I had a good one handy. His *vota em kella beksen* were so short already his ankles were sticking out. But then his eyes widened and he actually looked kind of surprised.

"I'm not laughing. I'm sorry. How –?" He laughed again. "Everybody's been looking all over the place for you!"

You bet he was laughing, but maybe only because he was glad to see us. He didn't seem to give a care how disgusting we looked. He didn't ask us a pile of questions even. He just took our bikes and set them against a tree. Then he held his hand out to Lena. "You'd better come inside once. You look like you could maybe use something to eat."

I couldn't help it, I started crying my eyes out. Right there in front of Mark Giesbrecht, who sure didn't seem one bit like the Mark Giesbrecht I knew. He didn't call me a wimp or say a word about it. He just went about helping Lena limp to the house, with me walking beside trying to stop snivelling like a baby.

I knew things couldn't be the same between us after that. I just wasn't sure yet if they'd changed for better or for worse.

For another thing, the police weren't done with us. There had been no end of fuss when they drove up to the Giesbrecht's farm. Dad had jumped out of the car while it was still moving yet. He'd grabbed Lena and me, giving us each a one-armed, headlock kind of hug, holding on tight without saying anything at first. There was someone else in the backseat, too. For a second I got my hopes up that it was maybe Mom. Then Beth got out and came running around the car. As soon as Dad let go she swept Lena up in her arms. "You're okay, right? They said you were okay. You're not hurt or anything? Oh, look at your leg!"

"We're fine," I said. "Just tired and sore."

"I need a bath," announced Lena.

And then everyone was crying and laughing and hugging and praising God all at the same time. And in the middle of it yet, the police were trying to ask questions.

Then above the din, Lena piped up. "A bad man followed us. But he didn't get us."

Just like that it got awful quiet. No one was smiling anymore. Mrs. Giesbrecht put her hand over her mouth.

"What do you mean, a man followed you?" asked one of the cops. And then people were all talking at once again and asking about the guy and what he looked like and what kind of truck he was driving and everything. I was trying to tell them what had happened, about how he'd waited at the farmyard and the bull had protected us and everything, and Lena was making sure I didn't leave out anything. She got more and more flushed, and made less and less sense, and hung on to Dad tighter and tighter all the time.

Finally Dad growled, "That's enough. My girls need to go home."

The police said they would finish getting our statements after we'd rested up a bit from our ordeal. So we left our bikes at the Giesbrechts to pick up later and the police gave us a ride home. Only first they made us stop at the hospital to get checked out. Dad thought that was a pretty good idea, too. The doctor cleaned up Lena's scrapes.

"They're a little dehydrated, but otherwise no worse for wear," he said. "Make sure they drink lots of fluids and get plenty of rest for the next few days."

That sounded okay by me. By the time we got home, I was too bushed to do anything but fall into bed. I barely had time to wonder when the bomb was going to drop and how big an explosion it would be, and then I was asleep already.

There was still something else yet that wasn't anywhere near normal. My family wasn't acting like my family. No one was being loud. No one was yelling at anyone.

While we were sleeping, Grandma Redekop had made roast chicken with *bubbat* for supper, because Beth told her how it was my favorite. My favorite was really lasagna like I'd had one time at Jillian's house, but I was pretty sure Grandma didn't know how to make lasagna and anyways, it was nice of Beth to remember for once that I liked *bubbat*, and for Grandma to cook a special supper and everything.

So I said, "Thanks, Grandma." And I gave her a kiss on her cheek.

"*Och vaut!*" Grandma hustled me out of her way and to the table. "Sit you *doy*, O'Lloyd," she said. She was blushing and everything.

Beth had made Lena's favorite, which was angel food cake with seven-minute rainbow frosting, which Mom usually only made for birthdays.

I started to wonder if we were in someone else's house or if aliens had maybe taken over our family. Beth ran hot baths for us after supper – one for each, so we didn't even have to share the water. She put clean sheets on our beds and everything. Dad came upstairs to tuck us in like he used to when we were still little. I figured for sure now our luck had run out and the bomb was about to drop. Dad was awful quiet, as if the explosion that was coming was so big, it was still working up steam.

But instead of exploding, all Dad did was tell us how disappointed he was that we could be so irresponsible. He talked so soft that I felt way worse yet than if he'd torn a strip off us. At least if he'd yelled, then I could've been mad back at him. Now I could only feel lousy for making everyone worry so much and for doing something so reckless that might have ended up a lot worse than it did.

This was one time Reverend Funk's sermon about using soft answers to turn away wrath really worked.

Dad made us promise that we would never go off anywhere alone, and never ever go anywhere unless adults knew where we were and all that. But he didn't ground us.

Grown-ups can be hard to figure out. But what I was thinking, while I was brushing wet paint on the siding, was that maybe the reason Dad didn't ground us was because he felt bad, too. I think he felt bad about giving

Tommy away. Not grounding us this once was his way of making it up to us. Plus he was pretty happy that we were all in one piece and everything.

Dad never did come right out and say he was sorry about Tommy. But I knew he was. He'd taken the whole rest of the week off work, hadn't he? He was at the other end of the scaffolding right now helping me paint, wasn't he?

The biggest thoughts spinning around in my head, the most important ones, right there in the middle of all the other thoughts spinning around, were about Mom. They were the most anxious thoughts, too, the kind that made my stomach feel sick.

"Daddy," Lena had whispered last night, half asleep before Dad finished talking. "Is Mommy mad at us?"

Dad smiled and said something in Plautdietsch. "Of course she's not mad at you, *schnigglefritz*. Whatever gave you that idea?"

What else should she think? No one had even said anything about Mom.

Lena pushed herself up on her elbow. "Then how come she didn't come with to get us?"

Exactly. I had the same question as Lena, but I'd already guessed what the answer was. I'd already guessed that if a person was getting shock treatments, they probably didn't just let them walk out in the middle of it. Not even if their kids were missing.

"Mom wants to come home," Dad sighed. "But she has to get better first. She'll be home soon, you'll see."

Soon. *Fuy.* I was tired of hearing that word. It didn't mean anything.

Lena didn't think much of it either. "But maybe she's forgot about us," she said.

"Mom could never forget about you."

I could've told him different.

Dad chewed on his lip when he was thinking just like Lena did all the time. "It's just that, at the hospital they give her that special medicine, remember? But the medicine needs some time to work. So we have to be patient. We have to help Mom by taking care of things at home so she doesn't worry about us so much, until the medicine has time to work. And then she'll come home again."

It was a long speech for Dad. Lena lay down again and pulled the covers under her chin.

"If you want, we can go see Mom tomorrow."

Lena nodded.

"But we won't tell her about your adventure yet," Dad added. "We'll wait until she gets home, okay?"

"Okay."

Dad kissed her forehead and put out the light. "Now say your prayers and go to sleep, *schnigglefritz*. You're all worn out."

And then I got it. Dad hadn't told Mom we were gone even. I mean, what could she have done anyways? Except worry. If she got all worried, then maybe they'd have to give her more shock treatments or pills or something, and then it would be still longer before she came home.

And now we were back safe and sound, there was no point in getting her all worked up over it.

All of that made perfect sense. But it didn't make me feel any better.

I had to smarten up already. We were doing okay. Lena and I had Dad and Beth and Grandma and Auntie Nettie. And each other. Who did Mom have in that place?

Mom was the one who needed someone to rescue her.

Leave it in God's hands, Reverend Funk had said.

Uy uy uy. In between all the other thoughts were a ton of thoughts about God, running around in my head like chickens with their heads cut off. I couldn't even keep track of all the questions, never mind think what the answers might be.

The thing was, I didn't know anymore what I believed, whether I really didn't believe in God, or whether I did. Mostly I didn't want to think about it right then. One thing at a time, and right now, the most important thing to think about was Mom.

So I pretended to shove all my thoughts and questions about God up in a closet; I shoved them all in there and closed the door.

I tried to concentrate on painting. I liked dipping my brush in the creamy paint. I liked how the paint glided on with long smooth brush strokes, and how the roller spread the paint into the grain of the wood. I was getting the hang of using the exact right amount and not too much, so it wouldn't run or drip.

Just like that, the siding was brand-new again. Painting hid all the nicks and bumps, all the places where the siding wasn't perfect. Too bad there wasn't a paintbrush to use on people.

All morning already while we were painting, Lena had been bugging Dad to take her to see Mom. Now Dad started getting cleaned up and said it was time to go. But I kept right on painting.

"You should get yourself cleaned up a bit for Mom, *meyahl*," Dad said.

Soon I was going to have to go back to Eden. I knew that. Soon, but not yet. Not today. "Can I go later?" I asked. "By myself?"

Dad didn't look too happy about it, but he nodded. "Beth can give you a ride over tonight or tomorrow, if that's what you want. Don't wait too long, though. Mom's been asking about you."

"She has?" I didn't mean to act so surprised. Only I was sort of relieved. I mean, if she was asking about me, at least that meant she remembered who I was.

"Of course." Dad looked at me curiously. "Are you sure you don't want to come with?"

"I'm kinda tired. I just want to take it easy this afternoon, you know, like the doctor said."

He couldn't very well argue with that.

For once I did take it easy, too, just like I said I would. Except for the five minutes it took for me to run down to the Co-op and get this week's paper after promising

Beth fifty times that I was only going across the street and back. I checked the weather forecast. Partly cloudy most of the week with evening showers, but by Friday clearing again.

Friday night it was, then. I had two days still, to figure out a plan.

23

Come over when you have nothing on

First thing after breakfast the next day the police came over. They asked Lena and me a bunch of questions about the man who had followed us, and what kind of truck he was driving and everything.

Lena remembered the truck was brown with lots of dents and rust, and that the back had a white top on it. "It was old."

"Do either of you remember the make, or the model? Was it a Ford or a Chevy or a GM?" asked one of the cops.

Like we would know the difference. But there was one thing I did know. "The license was ADP something."

The officer stopped writing to look up at me. "You know that for sure? You actually remember the license plate?"

"The first three letters. Yeah." My face was getting hot. The first three letters of the license plate were the same as Aaron's initials – Aaron David Penner. I used to scribble them in my notebook at school all the time. But no way was I telling that to the police, or anyone else either. "They were ADP. I'm positive. And I'm pretty sure there was a five in the last three numbers."

The officer grinned, making a note in his book. "That's going to be a big help."

"Do you think he was really after us?" I asked.

"We'll know more after we find him and talk to him. But from the way he hung around at the farm for so long . . . I'd say you girls did the right thing, running away."

All of a sudden I was almost glad I wasn't allowed out by myself for a while yet.

"*Nah yo*," Dad said after the police left. "That's over. There's a couple of paintbrushes with our names on them."

But before going outside to paint, I did something I never thought I'd ever do in a million years.

I phoned up Mark Giesbrecht.

Anyways, it was Beth's idea. She thought I should phone to say thank you to him and his mom for being so nice to me and Lena. I mean, his mom had called Dad and let us clean up in their bathroom and made us pancakes, and his dad had dropped off our bikes for us and everything. The least I could do was phone to say thanks.

First I talked to Mrs. Giesbrecht. She was nice, and awful happy that Lena and I were okay. She called Mark to the phone and I thanked him yet, too.

"No problem," he said.

Then out of the blue he said, "Do you want to come over to our house some time to ride horses?"

I was so stunned I didn't answer. So the phone line was pretty much quiet for a bit and then Mark kept on talking some more.

"Uh, how about Sunday afternoon maybe? You know, if you have nothing on and it fits."

I could almost hear him groaning and I knew he had said in English what he was thinking in Plautdietsch and for sure it wasn't the same. But I knew already what he meant to say before he added, "I-I mean, if you're not doing anything."

I still didn't know what to say. So I said, "Sure, okay."

"Bring Lena with, if she wants."

"Sure. Okay." My brain was stuck.

Imagine that. Me going horseback riding with Mark Giesbrecht.

Uy uy uy.

"What was that all about?" Beth asked when I hung up.

What was I going to tell her? I couldn't very well keep it a secret. I was going to need a ride over there. So I made it sound like no big deal. Because it wasn't. "Nothing," I said. "I'm going horseback riding on Sunday. At Mark's."

Beth raised one eyebrow. "All right, little sister. Your first date."

Date? Who said anything about a date? I rolled my eyes so Beth would know how ridiculous she was being.

"We're just friends. We're just going to ride horses. And he invited Lena, too."

Beth was grinning like the Cheshire cat. "Yeah, sure."

"*Hmmph.*" I turned on my heel and headed outside to paint. Dad and I had got a lot done yesterday, and with two of us working again, we might even finish the first coat this morning.

Anyways, it didn't count as a date if your little sister came with. Did it?

The second Jillian came coasting up the back sidewalk after lunch I ducked out the door to meet her. Maybe it was because I was so happy to see her, and that's why the thing I was thinking just popped out of my mouth.

"I'm sorry!" Both of us blurted out the same thing at once.

Then we both broke up laughing yet, too.

We had so much to catch up on, neither of us remembered even to say what it was we were sorry for. It didn't make any difference. Making up was so easy I wondered how come it had taken me this long to get around to it.

Right away Jillian and I rode over to Sadie's. I didn't beat around the bush. I came right out and told her I was sorry about running out on her at the pool that night. Saying sorry didn't seem so scary anymore, not after everything that had happened the last couple of days.

"It was a lousy thing to do," I said, "even if I was scared. And kind of jealous, you know, that Aaron liked you instead of me. But I'm over that now, and I'm really sorry. Can we be friends again?"

Sadie started bawling, so it was almost impossible to understand a word she was trying to say. Finally, when she calmed down a bit, I found out that she wasn't really mad even about getting ditched.

"I probably would've done the same," she sniffed. "Everything happened so fast." Sadie said she was the one jealous of me, because I was never scared of anything and was better at stuff like swimming and diving. Which was pretty funny when you thought about it, because most of the time I felt like I was scared of everything.

Sadie said she was afraid Aaron would dump her for me and that's why she'd given me the cold shoulder. "I'm sorry, Elsie. Now Aaron doesn't like me anymore anyways. He broke up with me!" And she started bawling all over again.

Aaron, that moron, had told Sadie he wanted to play the field. As if in Hopefield there was so much to pick from.

"His loss," said Jillian, fiercely, after we finally got Sadie to stop crying. "What a *schozzle!*"

Then I knew she'd been listening to Pete again because I didn't know even what a *schozzle* was. Still, it sounded like it fit Aaron pretty good.

Holy Moses. We'd gone and wasted practically half our summer over a stupid guy. That really cracked us up. Talk about *schozzles.*

At the pool everyone was all over me to tell them about what happened. So I had to tell the whole story all over again. They laughed themselves silly at the part about the bull chasing us up a tree. Everyone except Mark.

"Good thing you stayed put," he said. "That old bull would as soon rip you to shreds as look at you. He'd have run right over that guy if he'd come into the pasture after you."

I wasn't used to this Mark. I figured he'd be itching to tell all about what a blubberface I was when Lena and I showed up at his farm. For sure they'd all get a good laugh out of that.

Instead, here he was sticking up for me. I wasn't the only one who noticed either. Jillian poked me in the ribs.

"What?" I hissed.

She rolled her eyes, grinning, so I knew exactly what she was thinking.

Even Aaron was impressed that we'd spent the night in an abandoned farmhouse. Only I didn't seem to care so much anymore what Aaron thought.

I never said anything about waking up in the night and seeing the ghosts and the stars. That part was mine.

"Weren't you scared?" Naomi shuddered. "All alone at night like that?"

"Witless," I nodded. "But we were too *ootyepoopt* to think too much about how scared we were."

"*Ootyepoopt?*" howled Jillian.

"You know. Wiped out. Pooped."

That cracked her up a good one.

"But what if that creep had come back to look for you?" Heather shuddered.

"He didn't," I shrugged, like it was no big deal, only the goose pimples crawled across my skin. Even riding to the pool with Heather and Sadie I was checking every truck that drove by or was parked in the parking lot.

"God was watching over you," said Joy. Which was what Beth and Auntie Nettie and Grandma and Dad had said, too. And Mrs. Giesbrecht and the doctor and one of the cops even.

Maybe they were right. Maybe there was a God watching over Lena and me and that's how come the man went away without coming into the pasture after us. It didn't make sense that God would first send a stranger to scare us and then save us from him. What kind of joke would that be?

Part of me sort of liked the idea that if there was a God, he would be the kind of God who would look out for people whether they believed in him or not. But then why would God take care of some people and not others? I mean, bad things happened to good people every day.

I just didn't get how come God got to decide who would get hurt and who wouldn't. Who would be sick, and who wouldn't. Who would be rich and who wouldn't. Who would be beautiful and who wouldn't. Who would die today and who wouldn't.

If there was no God, then there was no one to be mad at when bad things happened. You just had to live with what came your way and make the best of it. Or not. It was up to you. It was sort of scary to think like that, like we were all alone in the world with no one but ourselves to watch out for us. But it was a lot easier to understand.

Except for one thing. Except for the way I felt at that old farmyard that night, standing under the stars. I didn't feel like I was all alone then. I felt like I was part of something big, big as the whole universe. Something wonderful.

And that made me feel braver than I'd ever thought I could be.

"I can't believe you'd go to all that trouble for a scraggy old alley cat," Aaron shook his head.

"I can," said Jillian, still laughing so hard she had to wipe the tears from her eyes. "I think it was a perfectly noble thing to do. We should put up posters, all over town."

Posters. Why hadn't I thought of that?

"Someone will have seen him, you bet," Sadie nodded. "You can't give up hope."

So we agreed to meet at my place in the morning to make posters. And I would tell Jillian and Sadie about my idea, I decided. I'd ask for their help.

For sure I was going to need it.

❧

That night before I went to bed I was checking out how hairy my legs were already, and thinking I should maybe shave them again. If I went horseback riding with hairy legs, Mark might say something again about loaning me a swather. I mean, if he helped me up into the saddle or something. He seemed different from before, when he'd made that joke, but probably it would be a good idea not to lead him into temptation.

Besides which, I'd read in one of Beth's Chatelaine magazines that women should shave their legs once a week at least.

Only problem was, I felt guilty about using Beth's razor without asking. It was okay before when Beth was being such a bossy old bag, but now, when she was being almost nice, it didn't feel right anymore.

Anyways, the light was on in her bedroom so I knew she was reading in there. I knocked, waiting until she said to come in. I didn't go all the way in. I stood in the doorway in case I had to make a quick getaway.

"Do you think it might be all right for me to use your razor?"

"What?" Her nose stayed stuck in her book.

"Do you think it might be all right if I used your razor? You know, to shave my legs."

Beth's eyes and nose appeared above the top of her book. "You're going to ride horses, not going to a prom."

Right away my cheeks began to get hot.

"Why in heaven's name would you want to shave your legs? You're twelve."

That was the problem with being honest. You have to do it all the time. "Promise you won't laugh?"

"Yeah, yeah."

So I told her about Mark's joke about lending me a swather.

She didn't laugh. She put down her book. "You sure you want to bother with this guy? If you ask me he sounds like a first-class idiot."

I nodded. "Yeah. Only, I don't think he's so much of an idiot as I thought before. Sometimes he can be almost nice even."

Beth rolled her eyes. "It's your funeral. C'mon, you'll slice yourself to shreds if you try it alone." And then she looked at the scabs healing on my shins and ankles and I could see she was putting two and two together. But she only shook her head and marched me downstairs to the bathroom.

She gave me a new razor blade, and let me use her shaving cream and showed me how to run the razor over my leg real light, in slow smooth strokes. "Like this. You don't have to press hard, and don't be in a hurry or you'll nick yourself for sure. And be careful around your ankles especially."

Lying in bed later feeling my smooth legs against the sheets, I was thinking Beth was maybe not so much of an idiot as I thought before either.

24

It helps nothing just to pucker the lips

"Voh scheent et, meyahles?" Dad grabbed Lena when he came down for breakfast, giving her a whisker rub until she squealed and giggled and squirmed to get loose.

He headed for me and Beth, too, but I ducked and Beth warded him off with a spoonful of waffle batter. Waffles, on a week day. That's one thing conditions never favored. I definitely liked the new Beth better. Only I wondered how long she was going to stick around.

"How come you're in such a good mood this morning?" she asked Dad.

Dad chuckled. "Look once what I found." He went into the porch and came out holding something behind his back. "I thought Lena could do with a playmate." And he plopped a little black-and-white fur ball on her lap.

My father. A kitten.

Wonders never cease, says my mom.

Lena let out a terrific squeal. So did the kitten. It scrambled across the kitchen table, knocking over the milk carton. Milk spilled over the table and dribbled off the edge onto Dad's shoes.

Dad lifted one foot. Milk dripped from his shoe to the floor. "What is it with me and cats?" he said.

I scooped up the kitten and handed it back to Lena. Everyone agreed it was adorable. Tommy would have thought it silly, though. Too silly to be worth a glance. My heart hurt, a little stabbing hurt, whenever I thought about Tommy. I couldn't help it. The kitten was cute, but I missed that old tom still.

Lena cuddled the kitten against her cheek. "I can keep it? Really?"

Dad nodded. "You feed it, you clean the litter box and it has to have its shots and get fixed when it's old enough. That's all I need is a litter of kittens yet."

He didn't fool me. Or Lena. Her face lit up like a Christmas tree. "Thank you, thank you, thank you!"

"You can thank Elsie's boyfriend. It was his idea."

The milk I was drinking practically sprayed out my nose. "My boyfriend?!"

"Giesbrecht's Mark, the one with the hair that makes him look like a sheepdog," grinned Dad. He was getting a real kick out of this. "He phoned up, said they were looking for homes for their kittens. He thought Lena maybe would like one. Then I think he said something about the two of you going horseback riding?"

"He's not my boyfriend. He invited Lena, too. Sounds like Lena's the one he likes. She's the one who got the kitten." The more I talked the redder I got. The more I talked the more Dad and Beth laughed. Jumping Jehoshaphat. The only thing I could do was shut up.

"I don't know," Beth wheezed. "I think Dad's right. Elsie has a boyfriend."

"Elsie and Mark," chanted Lena, "sitting in a tree –"

"Grow up, *knirps*." I tackled my little sister, wrestling her to the floor. She didn't put up a fight even, she was so busy laughing. Only the kitten didn't think much of all the commotion. It squirmed out of Lena's arms and bolted across the kitchen floor, right under the broom leaning next to the back door. The broom toppled over, hit the counter, and knocked over a glass. The glass rolled right off the counter, hit the floor, and burst into a million pieces.

Dad laughed harder than ever. Beth doubled over. All *knippsing* Lena's nose got me was more squeals and giggles.

Fuy. I gave up. This family was more like the family I was used to. Loud and obnoxious. Funny thing was, I thought maybe I liked them this way.

"Domino," giggled Lena. "I'm going to call my kitten Domino."

❧

That afternoon Sadie, Jillian, and I plastered posters all over town – at the Co-op, library, town hall, post office,

Janzen's Variety, Rexall Drugs, Driedger's Photography, the Credit Union, and the Harvester, which pretty much covered Main Street from one end to the other. Then we put more up at the pool and on all seven bulletin boards at all seven Mennonite churches, and even the Lutheran Church yet, too.

Dad shook his head but let us do what we wanted. Grandma rolled her eyes and muttered, "What do you want with that old *kohta*?"

Only Auntie Nettie smiled and said, "You go right ahead and keep looking. It helps nothing just to pucker the lips, you have to whistle, not?" Which is what Mom always said when Lena and I promised to clean our room and then never did.

Beth even gave us a ride out to TK's drive-in on the highway, so we could put a poster up there, too. And then she drove us along the country roads between town and Nickel Enns' farm, so we could have one last look for Tommy.

And when we had one poster left, Jillian said we should put it up at Eden, and maybe stop in to say hi to my mom. I'd finally got around to telling them where Mom was and what I planned to do about it. The minute they'd arrived to make posters that morning, I'd dragged them upstairs to my room and shut the door. Good thing Lena was busy playing with Domino so I didn't have to worry about her spying on us. Just to make sure, I checked under the beds.

"What's up?" Jillian demanded. She flopped on my bed. "You're like a Mexican jumping bean."

That's exactly how I felt, too, like my insides were full of jumping beans. I took a deep breath. "Okay. Here's the thing. I have to get my mom out of Eden for a couple of hours."

Right away Jillian and Sadie looked at each other. For almost three weeks already my mom had been in that place and this was the first I'd said anything to them about it. But I could see on their faces that they knew already.

"It has to be at night," I added. "Actually, it has to be tomorrow night." Might as well give them the whole scoop up front.

"Jeepers," breathed Sadie. "Why don't you break into Fort Knox while you're at it?"

But nothing fazed Jillian. "We'll have a pajama party at my place," she said. I could practically see her brain shifting into high gear. "Then it'll be easy to sneak out."

My knees went all weak like a dishrag. I sank to the floor, cross-legged. "So you don't think I'm totally crazy?"

"Of course you are. Crazy and brilliant." Jillian hugged her knees against her chest, looking at me all thoughtful like. "I wasn't sure what to say before, you know, about your mom. I thought you didn't want to talk about it."

"I didn't, I guess." *Uy.* This was something I hadn't counted on, but if my friends were going to help out and everything, they probably deserved to know what was going on. "Sometimes Mom . . . gets sort of lost. She gets sad. It's hard to explain."

It was hard to think of the right words, especially when I wasn't sure what I was trying to say even. And then I didn't have to.

"It doesn't matter," said Jillian. "What I'd really like to know is what are we going to do once we get her out?"

I pulled my feet up into a lotus position which was the only yoga position I knew, and breathed deep. Now for sure they were going to think I was crazy.

"Take her out to the country and show her the stars," I said, looking them straight in the eyes.

Mom needed to see the stars. Not the way they looked when they started to come out at night. Not the way they looked in town. She needed to see the stars at two in the morning, when the sky was full to bursting. When all those gazillions of stars shining in the heavens made everything else seem . . . like not such a big deal. Not because the stars made a person feel small and unimportant. It was like, the opposite.

For sure you were small. But the universe was huge and glorious and somehow, you were connected up to that. It was almost like there was a power in being part of something so glorious, a power that gave a person hope. That made anything and everything seem possible.

"Show her the stars?" Sadie didn't get it.

I knew she wouldn't. Neither would Jillian. How could they, unless they'd seen it for themselves? I nodded. "Yep."

"Couldn't she just look out her window?"

"Nope," I shook my head. "It's not the same." I didn't try to explain. Either they were going to help me, or they weren't.

First thing, we had to get Mom out of Eden. In the middle of the night. Then out into the country where there were no lights. And it had to be a clear night. Tomorrow, when it was supposed to stop raining and the new moon wouldn't be so big yet it would drown out all the stars.

Anyways, that was my idea. If I had the guts to go through with it. Taking off to look for Tommy was one thing. Kidnapping my own mother was something else again. I could hardly believe I was thinking about it, never mind that I was going to do it yet.

It helps nothing just to pucker the lips, I thought, *you have to whistle.*

Remembering that made me feel better again. An idea wasn't any good unless you did something about it, not?

Jillian slid off the bed to sit beside me. "Anything we can do to help, we'll do it."

"For sure," said Sadie.

"Okay," I nodded. "Here's what I was thinking . . ." Their grins got bigger and bigger as they helped to work it all out.

❧

"What are you going to tell her?" Sadie blurted out in the car, after Jillian said we should go visit my mom.

Jillian jabbed her hard in the ribs with an elbow and I hissed at her under my breath.

"What do you have to tell Mom about?" Beth frowned at us in the rearview mirror and we wiped the grins off our faces. Never mind how nice Beth was being lately, she wasn't going to go for letting us sneak out in the middle of the night.

"Nothing," I said, thinking fast. "For sure not about Tommy. I don't think I'll tell her that he's missing. Just in case he still comes back yet."

Beth shook her head. "That's not going to happen. You know that, don't you?" But she didn't say it in a mean way. She said it like she was a little sorry even. "Stopping to see Mom is a good idea, though. You did promise Dad."

This wasn't how I'd planned it. What would I do if Mom didn't know who I was, never mind recognize my friends?

But there was no way out. Before I knew it Beth, Jillian, and Sadie had swept me through the front door. Beth marched right in like she owned the place. Mom was awake, sitting in a chair in her room.

Beth stooped to kiss her forehead. "Hi, Mom. We brought you some flowers."

"They're lovely," Mom smiled. "Thank you."

Beth grabbed a water glass from the table and arranged the wildflowers we'd picked. "I'll just get some water for them." She raised her eyebrows at me on her way to the bathroom. "Are you coming in or not?"

I didn't realize I was standing in the doorway still. Behind me Sadie gave a little cough. Jillian nudged me forward. I took three quick steps across the room to give Mom a kiss.

"Hello, sweetheart," she smiled. "It's been so long since I've seen you. You're browner, and taller!"

"I'm not any taller than last week, Mom."

"Oh, I don't know." She winked and gave me a one-arm hug. "And look who you've brought with you!"

Mom seemed better, that's for sure. At least she wasn't so mixed up as last time. I couldn't tell, though, if she was really cheerful, or if she was faking it.

"They've finally opened your window for you," I said.

"It's been so terribly hot the last few nights. Most of us have started to sleep with our doors and windows open because of the heat. Anything to get a breeze."

"We'll ask Dad to get you a fan," said Beth, returning with the flowers.

"What do you do all day in here?" Jillian asked, looking around the room and frowning.

Yikes, what a question! I winced inside. I'd never had the guts to ask that question and here it had just popped out of Jillian. But Mom laughed.

"Well," she said. "I go to group, and to craft time."

"You do crafts?" Sadie laughed.

"We sew leather wallets together," Mom nodded. "It's quite an artform." Then she winked, grinning. "I hate it! Oh, how I hate it!"

"Why do it then?" I asked.

"Because," she shrugged, "I keep thinking that if I play along like a good patient and pretend to enjoy it, then maybe they'll let me go home sooner!"

We all laughed, and after that visiting was easy. I didn't tell Mom anything about our plans, though. I couldn't, not with Beth right there. Anyways, even if Beth hadn't been with us, I didn't have a clue what I would've said.

"Your mom doesn't look sick," Jillian whispered to me as we left. "Not, you know, like some of the other people in here."

I hesitated, and then blurted, "Sometimes I think if she stays here too long, she'll maybe turn into one of those robots."

Jillian nodded. "Yeah. But don't worry." She grinned, throwing her arm around my shoulders. "Your mom's too cool to let that happen."

I was too surprised to say anything. My mom? Cool?

ॐ

We were in the middle of eating supper when the police showed up at our door again. It was the same cop who'd asked us all the questions before. At first I thought he had more questions for us, only he didn't.

Instead he told us how another little girl from the next town had disappeared while she was riding her bike in the park. She'd gone missing that same morning.

Good thing we were all sitting down already. My chest got so tight when the cop told us that, I could hardly breathe. My friends and I sometimes rode our bikes to that town to play in that park. It had the best climbing tree in all of southern Manitoba.

Almost right after the girl was reported missing, he said, the police had stopped a truck like the one Lena and I had told them about. The truck's license plate was ADP 358.

"You were right about that license number," he nodded at me.

And in the back of the truck, what do you think? The police found the girl. Her name was Melody. She was younger even than Lena. The man had Melody tied up so she couldn't run away, and he'd taped her mouth, so she couldn't yell for help or anything.

My insides felt like they'd melted and drained away, thinking about how scared Melody must have been. She was okay now though, the cop said. At least, she was back home with her family. They'd found her before anything even worse happened. And the man who took her was in jail. This time everything had turned out okay.

"We had nothing else to go on," the police officer told Dad. "If it wasn't for your daughters' description, we would never have been looking for that truck."

I guess going to look for Tommy wasn't all for *nusht* after all. Not for Melody, it wasn't.

Something like that makes you think, that's for sure.

25

A blind hen also finds a good kernel

riday morning right off the bat, Dad put the kibosh in our plan.

"No sleepovers. No bloody way," he said flatly. "Not after what's happened. Not at Jillian's or Sadie's or anyone else's house either."

"But, the guy was caught, Dad!"

"I said no, Elsie. If you have to have a sleepover, you can have your friends over here."

My jaw dropped. Never in my wildest dreams would I have ever imagined Dad letting me have friends over without Mom around. I don't think he knew what he'd said even until after he'd said it.

I made an emergency phone call to Jillian. "Now what are we going to do?"

Jillian thought a minute. "Time to call in the troops," she said. "Invite everyone for a pajama party, like your

Dad said. With so many of us, your Dad won't notice you're missing. And if he does, we'll just say you're in the bathroom or went to get something or whatever."

A few days ago I would've gone along with it, no problem. But I wasn't so crazy anymore about lying to my Dad. "I don't want anyone to have to lie," I said. "Eleanor and Joy couldn't lie even if they tried, which they wouldn't."

"Okay. We won't lie. Like I said, if we're careful we probably won't have to."

I wasn't so sure as Jillian. It sounded to me like a lot of people would maybe have to bear false witness to make this plan work. If not actually lying, for sure we'd be pulling the wool over Dad's eyes. Whether God was watching or not, I didn't like it. Only I couldn't think of a better idea.

There was still Lena to deal with yet. She wasn't going to be so easy to get rid of.

"If you can't beat 'em, join 'em," said Jillian.

So we told Lena she could come to the party if she wanted. Her face lit up.

"On one condition," I added. "You have to help us with a secret mission. Which means you can't say a word to Beth or Dad about what we do at our party."

"I won't," she promised. "Cross my heart and hope to die."

Fuy. It wasn't enough that I was going down the road

to hell, now I was dragging my little sister with me, too. I could hardly believe how far and how fast I'd fallen.

If there was a God, I was toast for sure.

꧂

All the way while I was riding to Eden that evening, and even while I was stashing my bike in the bushes, I was still wondering what kind of *mouse* I was stirring up for myself now. I was wishing I was back on my front porch camped out with all my friends. Only thing was, camping out with my friends wouldn't do too much of anything for Mom. It helps nothing just to pucker the lips, I reminded myself.

Anyways, at least the police had caught that creep who liked to pick up little kids. Otherwise I might have been too chicken to do what I was doing.

I checked the watch I'd borrowed from Heather. We'd synchronized watches, Jillian and I, before I left. Visiting hours at Eden would last another hour yet. Plenty of time still. I strolled around the building and across the road to the service station, all the time trying to look cool, like I just wanted a soft drink and not like I was getting ready to kidnap my own mother.

Quite a few people were coming and going from Eden. I bought a Mountain Dew from the cooler and hung around, pretending I was checking out the candy bars. Sure enough, it didn't take too long before three people walked across the grounds to the service station. They came inside to buy smokes and pop. When they headed back, I followed them.

I followed them across the grounds, up the steps and right through the front door.

The nurse at the front desk was busy talking to someone. She nodded at us when we came in, but I don't think she really noticed me that much because I made sure to keep the others between me and her. Not that it would have made a diff, if she did see me I mean. But I wanted to stay inconspicuous, just in case.

After that it was pretty easy. I ducked through the lounge and down the hall to Mom's room like always. Outside her open door I stopped, going over in my head one more time what I was going to tell her.

Good thing I didn't walk in right aways. I could hear someone in there, visiting with her. Not just someone. Dad. I couldn't tell what they were saying because they were talking Plautdietsch. Now what was I going to do? The plan was for me to hide in Mom's room. I never thought about what would happen if Mom had visitors, never mind Dad yet!

I checked the time again. Dad probably wouldn't leave until visiting hours were over. The game would be over before it started if I was wandering the hallways when the nurses came around to check up on everyone.

A drop of sweat trickled down my face. Mom was right. It was crazy hot in here. I couldn't think right, it was so hot. I slipped away quietly, back to the lounge again. It was a little cooler in here at least.

What I needed was another place to hide. Think, *meyahl*! I wandered around, pretending I was waiting for someone. Funny thing was, no one paid me too much attention. It was almost like I wasn't there. The patients watching TV had their backs to me. The other people in the room were mostly visiting with each other. The robot patients sitting here and there or shuffling around, they never even saw me.

I leaned against the upright piano in the corner, wondering if maybe I was invisible. So it goes. When you're a kid, grown-ups look right past you. Which tonight, for once, was a good thing.

The intercom crackled and spit. "Visiting hours will be over in five minutes."

For some reason, people look up always when there is an announcement over the intercom. I saw my chance and grabbed it. When everyone in the lounge looked over at the speaker on the wall, I slipped in behind the piano.

It was perfect. There was lots of room for a kid like me to hide, room enough to sit in the corner, even stretch my legs out if I wanted to. Now all I had to do was wait. I checked to see if my watch was working still. Three long hours of waiting to go. All the way till midnight.

From behind the piano I could hear people moving around, saying good-bye. Feet shuffled past. Then it got quiet for a long time. Just when I was thinking everyone had left and I could maybe breathe a little easier, I heard one more set of footsteps cross the room. And then the lights went out.

I hugged my knees closer.

❧

You'd think three hours hiding behind a piano would give a person plenty of time to think, to sort out stuff in their head. Only I found out it didn't work that way. Not if the whole time the person is too scared and too hot to think about anything except getting out of the place where they're hiding.

Every time there was a noise, I jumped.

One time the bushes scratched against the window nearby. First thing I thought it was a wild animal trying to get in, but then I figured out it was probably just a breeze outside. One time I heard tiny paws skittering over the tile and wondered if the people who worked here knew they had mice. One time I heard this real soft *click, click, click* – so soft I had to hold my breath to make sure I'd heard it. *Click, click, click.* After a long time I figured out that I was hearing the sound the second hand made as it moved around the clock on the wall over my head.

I counted up to five hundred seconds and might have counted still more, only then someone came into the room. I held my breath, listening to the footsteps shuffle around the room, wandering here and there. When I couldn't hold my breath any longer, I cupped my hands over my mouth and breathed as quietly as I could. The footsteps shuffled closer and closer, till whoever was in the room was standing right beside the piano.

A terrible urge came over me to jump up and run to home base and shout "home free!"

"You shouldn't be out of bed, Sally," a voice said, firmly. Maybe even a little sharply.

I caught my breath. It was a woman's voice; the night nurse. Almost I could hear her frowning. More footsteps marched across the room.

Sally. That was the girl we'd seen having the fit that day.

"I couldn't sleep," muttered Sally. "It's too *schindashin hite*."

Atta girl, I cheered silently. *You tell 'em, Sally.*

"There's no need for that kind of language." The nurse's voice was definitely sharp this time. "Come now. You have to stay in your room."

The nurse waited for Sally to shuffle back down the hall. Then she left, too.

I took a huge breath, hugged my knees tight to my chest and waited for my heart to stop hammering. My hiding place got still stuffier every minute until I was smothering already. I couldn't move, I couldn't breathe, I couldn't hardly think. Little beads of sweat collected on my upper lip, and the back of my neck felt cold and clammy. That funny ringing in my ears was back again. Pretty soon I was going to pass out yet.

If I passed out now, probably a janitor would find me in the morning, dead. Only then I thought some more about how the janitor probably never cleaned behind here and no one would find me at all until days later when my body started to decay and stink up the room.

I checked. No dust bunnies. So they did clean. What was I thinking? Cleanliness is next to godliness, not? At least they'd find me right away then, if I did pass out.

Now I was starting to get delirious. Sweating and gasping, I groped my way out from behind the piano, never even checking to see if the coast was clear. Never in my life had I been so glad just to have space to breathe. After a bit I calmed down again, enough to get my bearings.

The lounge wasn't too dark really, not like behind the piano. Light reached in the front windows from the parking lot and street. The exit signs glowed red on both sides of the room and the clock on the wall was lit up. Mostly though, light poured in from the front foyer. The doors on both sides of the lounge were wide open, just like during the day.

God must be with me. Or else it was just dumb luck or the heat that made them leave the lounge doors open for once. Now I knew what Mom meant when she said even a blind hen also finds a good kernel now and then. Maybe if I found a few more good kernels this half-baked plan might work.

Next thing I walked around a bit, working out some of the kinks from being scrunched up behind the piano for so long. Only every step I took my runners squeaked on the floor. So I took them off and crept silently in my socks. I checked to see if it was time to put the plan into action. Eleven thirty, Heather's watch said. A bit early still, but I didn't know for sure how long it would take for me to wake up Mom and convince her to come with. I didn't let myself think about what would happen if she said no.

I slid on my stocking feet, across the lounge and down the hall. Then I stopped again, because the first door I tried to pass was wide open. All along the hallway, most doors were open, because of how hot it was. What if someone was lying awake in one of those rooms and saw me go by?

For a long time I stood there, frozen to the wall, not hardly daring to breathe, trying to get up the guts to go by those open doors. Then I heard voices somewhere behind me, at the other end of the lounge. And then footsteps, coming my way.

I darted across the open doorway and down the hall, past one door after another. When I came to Mom's room, I grabbed the doorframe, and swung through the open door into her room, flattening myself against the wall. Mom was sound asleep. She never moved a muscle.

I was just in time. Footsteps followed me down the hall, pausing every few steps. Someone was doing a bed check or something. My eyes darted around the room, looking for a place to hide. The footsteps were coming closer. I dove under the bed, scrunching as far back as I could into the shadows.

Two legs in white shoes appeared in the doorway. Above me, Mom turned over in her sleep. The shoes took a step inside the room. And another. I sucked in my breath. For sure this was it. I was done for.

Then the shoes turned on their heels and left. I exhaled, but I didn't dare move a muscle except for the ones I needed to breathe with. I waited, listening. The footsteps went all the way to the end of the hall and finally disappeared. When I was sure no one was coming back, I wriggled out from under the bed and slowly, carefully, closed the door. Then finally I could breathe normally.

The lounge was a cool oasis compared to Mom's room. *Schindashin hite* was right. And dark, too, now that the door was closed. I felt my way to the window and quietly slid open the curtains so the lights from the parking lot outside gave some light to see by. Maybe Mom would be less startled if she could at least see me.

I sat carefully on the edge of her bed, hoping the movement might be enough to wake her up, seeing how she was getting more restless now. No such luck. For all I knew, they'd given her some kind of sleeping pill.

"Mom," I whispered. "Wake up." I put my hand on her shoulder and gently nudged her.

She mumbled under her breath but didn't wake up. I tried again. "Mom! Wake up!"

"*Vaut es daut?*" she muttered, rolling over, her eyes blinking like they were trying to open. "*Vaut es louse?*"

I swallowed. "Nothing's wrong, Mom. I'm sorry I scared you. It's me. Elsie."

"Elsie? What are you doing here!?" She struggled to sit up, still drowsy.

"*Shhhh!* Quiet, Mom. Please?" At least she knew me anyways. That was a relief.

"Is something wrong? What's happened –"

She sat up and flung off the sheet, looking around in a daze. This was all wrong. I hadn't meant to confuse her like this. Mom felt the night table for her glasses, only instead she knocked them to the floor. I scooped them up and handed them to her, helping her slip them on.

"Nothing's wrong, Mom. Honest. Everything's fine. Really."

Mom reminded me of Wendy, sitting on the edge of the bed in her nightie, with her bare legs and feet poking out. But Peter Pan wasn't going to come flying in the window to whisk us away. And I didn't have any fairy dust, though it sure would've come in handy about now.

"I want to show you something, Mom."

"It's still dark outside," she said, not really awake yet.

"Shhh! Yeah. It's nighttime." I rummaged through her dresser and found a pair of slacks and a summer blouse and shoved them into her hands. "You need to get dressed. I have to show you something."

"Funny time to show me something," she mumbled as she stumbled into the bathroom, clutching her clothes. For a minute I thought I was going to get away with it, that Mom was so groggy she would just do what I told her. Only then I guess she started to wake up because she stopped at the door and turned to me. "What's this all about young lady? Why am I getting dressed in the middle of the night?"

"I – It's like this –" I threw up my hands. "I can't explain, Mom. I have to show you. Please come with. I know it sounds crazy, but *please*." How was I going to talk Mom into going along with everything? Then I remembered all the adventures she'd taken me on when I was little. All the mud puddles we'd played in, the foxtails we'd pretended to swim in, the rain we'd danced in, and the butterflies we'd chased.

I could feel the sweat trickling down my face and chest. "I really seriously want you to come with me, Mom. It's my turn to take you on an adventure. Remember?"

"An adventure?" She stood there for what felt like forever, until I was thinking that maybe she couldn't remember, maybe all our adventures had been zapped out of her brain already. Only I hoped maybe one or two of them were still there yet. And then, the corners of her mouth smiled a little. "We haven't had one of those in a while. I'd better get dressed if we're going on an adventure."

I grinned, nodding. "Hurry."

While she dressed, I slipped my runners back on and peeked to see that the coast was clear. I checked my watch again. We had to get moving.

"The night-duty nurse isn't going to let us just walk out, you know," Mom said as she pulled on her socks and shoes.

"We've got that covered." At least I hoped we did. I hoped Jillian and Sadie had been able to get away. "Ready?"

Mom stood up straight and held her hand out to me. The two of us walked out, hand in hand, bold as could be. When we reached the lounge I pulled Mom around the outside of the room, out of view of the open doors on the other side.

"Stay here a minute, okay?" I whispered, leaving Mom pressed against the wall next to the exit. Crawling on my hands and knees, I peered around the corner.

The nurse sat behind the front desk, filling out some papers. I slowly pulled back and scrambled to my feet. Then I checked my watch one last time.

"Okay," I whispered. "In a couple of minutes someone is going to start banging on the door. When the nurse gets up to see what's going on, that's when we get out of here."

Mom looked doubtful. "I'm not sure this is such a good idea, *schnigglefritz*. We should wait and go on an adventure tomorrow maybe, during visiting hours. We can't –"

A terrific pounding on the front door cut her short. I could hear a muffled voice outside, yelling, "Help! Please help!"

Things started to happen. They started to happen fast.

That was one of the things about adventures, I remembered now. Once an adventure got started it kind of swept you along.

I heard a chair scrape back, and footsteps running to the door. I heard buttons being punched, which meant the doors were unlocked. Squeezing Mom's hand, I risked another peek around the corner.

The nurse stood in the doorway, holding the inside door half open. "Stop that racket this instant!" she hissed. "This is a hospital for goodness sake."

Jillian yanked the outside door open. "Please, you have to help! We were racing. My friend fell off her bike!"

The nurse peered around Jillian. "What in heaven's name are you kids doing out in the middle of the night?"

It wasn't working. The nurse wasn't budging. *Move, move*, I pleaded silently. *Before someone else comes along to check what all the racket is about.*

"I think she hit her head!" Jillian cried.

Someone screamed. Not just a scream. An ear-splitting shriek. Only one person I knew could scream like that. Lena. But Lena wasn't supposed to be here.

"Hurry!" another voice yelled from outside.

I recognized Heather's voice. What was going on? Sadie and Jillian were the only ones who were supposed to be out there. Heather sounded hysterical. She even had me wondering what could have gone wrong. Mom tried to push past me. I had to hold her back.

The nurse reacted the same as Mom.

"Don't move her!" she called, dashing outside.

"Now!" I ran with Mom to the front doors.

Outside, Jillian had grabbed the nurse's arm and was running with her across the parking lot to where Sadie lay sprawled on the pavement with everyone else huddled around. They'd chosen the perfect spot. Just beyond the light spilling from the front doors, and in the shadow of the weeping birch on the front lawn.

"Okay, the coast is clear."

I shoved open the inside door, but Mom didn't budge, not even when I tried pulling her along with me. It was like her shoes were all of a sudden glued to the floor. The next second, Lena popped out from behind some bushes. She ran around the railing and held the outside door open.

"Hurry up!" she whispered.

Mom's eyes almost jumped out of their sockets. "Would someone please tell me what's going on?"

"I'll explain everything," I promised. "As soon as we're out of here." And then I pulled on Mom's hand and Lena grabbed the other and we burst through the doors, into the night.

Across the parking lot, everyone was still crowded around Sadie. The nurse had her back to us. Anyways, Eleanor, Heather, Naomi, and Joy all stood behind her, shielding the front door from her view even if she did turn her head. On the other side of Sadie, Jillian was watching for me.

We didn't hang around to see what happened next.

Mom, Lena, and I ran down the walk and around the corner of the building. At least, Lena and I ran, pulling Mom along between us.

26

When the heart is full, the mouth overflows

Nine of us, with Mom in the middle, walked hand in hand in the dark along the top of the floodway toward the cemetery. It felt a bit like we were Jesus and his disciples, heading home after a hard day of performing miracles.

For sure this adventure wasn't turning out like I had planned. In the middle of explaining everything to Mom, my friends had come barreling across the floodway on their bikes.

"What?" Jillian grinned when they caught up to us. "You didn't think we were going to go home and let you have all the fun?"

"Some people," said Sadie.

"I'll never be able to explain this," Mom was shaking her head and looking like she maybe was going to change her mind. "That poor nurse. You must've terrified her. She's probably reporting the lot of you to the police right now."

I felt a little bad about tricking the nurse, too. "I promise I'll go apologize to her tomorrow. Just come with us, Mom."

"Please, Mrs. Redekop?" pleaded Jillian.

"*Nah yo*," said Mom, shaking her head. "I suppose I'll have to, if only to keep an eye on you girls."

My friends cheered, even though the idea of Mom keeping an eye on us was sort of funny when you thought about it.

I didn't think I wanted to double Mom on my bike, at least not in the dark. So we left our bikes and started walking. All we had to do now was cut through the cemetery back to the main road and walk far enough out of town to get away from the lights.

No one wanted to spend any more time in the cemetery than we had to. We hurried through, careful to stay on the paths and not walk on anybody's grave. I'd never been in a cemetery at night before. Even with so many of us together, it was a creepy place. We were all huddled so close together that when one of us jumped at a shadow, we all jumped.

Even after we were already out of the cemetery, I kept getting this shiver up my back like there was maybe something behind us, watching. I couldn't help looking back just in case we'd maybe made some of those dead people angry, disturbing their peace, and they were following us.

I didn't see any zombies, but we weren't a half mile out of town when I looked back again and saw headlights coming toward us.

"There's a car coming," I said.

"Hide!" someone squealed. I think maybe it was Eleanor.

We all dove into the ditch to hide, automatically. We flattened ourselves in the long grass and peered out.

Everyone except Mom, that is. She stood calmly by the side of the road.

"For heaven's sake, girls. I let you sneak me out of the hospital. I followed you through the cemetery in the dead of night. But I'm not going to hide in a ditch!"

Mom was the smart one anyways. Already the mosquitos were eating us alive.

The car pulled up beside us, stopping a few feet from Mom. Not just any car. Dad's car. So it goes always.

I stood, hauling Lena up with me. Car doors slammed. I couldn't see who it was because the headlights were blinding me. Then Dad came striding into the light. "Esther? Are you all right?"

"Mom?!" Beth was right behind him. "Elsie! Where's Lena?"

"Right here." Lena peered out from behind me.

Beth ran over and practically lifted her off the ground, she hugged her so hard. "How dare you scare us like that?! *Again!* We've been driving all over town looking

for you! Of all the bonehead stunts –" She stopped sput-
tering to hug Lena some more.

"What is going on?" Dad spoke quietly, between his
teeth.

Nah yo, I thought, and started talking. I've never talked
so fast before in my life, trying to explain about taking
Mom to see the stars and how I knew it would make her
feel better and how I just wanted to do something, anything, to help, especially since everything was mostly my
fault, and that I hadn't been able to find Tommy but I
really wanted to do this one thing for Mom, because
maybe it would help make things right again.

At first Dad kept trying to interrupt, but after awhile
he gave up. There wasn't much else he could do because
I never shut up or hardly stopped for a breath even.
Pretty soon stuff was coming out of my mouth that I
didn't know was in there, about how when Lena and
I spent the night at that abandoned farmhouse there was
something wonderful out there with us so I wasn't afraid
anymore. There was something in the stars and in the fog
and in the night and inside me even.

I kept on talking about how I knew in my heart of
hearts that if Mom could see what I did that night, it
would do her more good than any pills or treatments or
anything else the doctors could give her. And maybe
she'd feel happy again instead of sad. Even for a little
while. So we were taking Mom out to have a good look at

the stars, at the way they were in the middle of the night when there wasn't enough room in the sky to hold them all. When it feels like you could practically reach out and touch God, He's so close.

"I think it must've been God," I said. "That night Lena and I were lost."

I was more surprised than anyone. I guess I still believed in Him after all. Why else would I say all that stuff?

"Are you done?" Dad asked. It was hard in the dark to tell how mad he was.

I gulped. "Uh-huh." Without looking I knew my friends were there, standing behind me, swatting mosquitos. "I'm done."

"It's not all Elsie's fault, Mr. Redekop," Sadie stepped forward beside me. "It was my idea to pretend I was hurt so the nurse would open the doors."

"And it was my idea to have a pajama party at your place, so Elsie could sneak out and go hide inside Eden," added Jillian, standing there on my other side.

"And it was my idea for all of us to help make a division," Lena piped up, squeezing between me and Jillian.

"Diversion," Sadie whispered.

"I mean a diversion," said Lena.

Dad ran his hand through his hair. Pretty soon he wasn't going to have any hair left. "I think I've heard enough."

Only there was still a little more he had to listen to. Mom put her arm around my shoulders and said, clear as a bell, "Isaak, I know how all this must look. But, we're here now. I for one would like to see all those stars Elsie's so excited about. You can take me back to the hospital after." Then she said something else to Dad, too, only she said it in Plautdietsch.

All around me I could hear my friends suck in their breath, waiting.

"Everyone in the car," Dad growled. "Now."

How many kids do you think can fit in an old Chrysler New Yorker?

Eight in the backseat for sure, sitting on each others' laps. And Lena in front, sitting on Mom's lap. With one cat yet, Domino, curled up on Lena's lap.

"I didn't have the heart to leave him at home by himself," said Beth.

Once everyone was wedged in and the doors were shut tight, Dad sat in the driver's seat. He waited with both hands on the wheel and looked straight ahead. "Okay, Elsie," he said. "Where are we going?"

I practically leaped over the backseat to throw my arms around his neck. "It doesn't matter. We don't have to go far. Anywhere away from the lights."

He nodded, and started the engine. "I know a good place."

Mom reached over and touched his arm. He put his hand on hers and squeezed it once before pulling onto the road.

"I can't believe this is happening," said Beth. "You're certifiable, you know that, don't you?"

I grinned back at her. "Probably. It runs in the family."

❧

We stopped at a crossroads a little ways south of town. Mom said it was where her grandparents first lived when they came here from Russia. There was nothing left of the old village now, except a few trees beside the road.

Beth found a blanket in the trunk. She spread it on the grass in the shallow ditch. Naomi, Eleanor, Joy, and Heather sprawled out on their backs on the blanket to gaze up at the sky.

First thing Mom did was take off her socks and shoes. She said she needed to breathe and so did her toes. Mom and Dad sat on the trunk of the car, leaning against the back windshield. Sadie and Jillian sat on the hood. And on the roof, Beth and I lay back with Lena between us. Domino prowled across our stomachs.

For sure this wasn't anything like I planned. But we'd made it. We were here, out in the country under the stars in the middle of the night. Nothing else could go wrong now.

Only the weather.

For the first little while clouds kept blocking the view of the stars so you couldn't see the whole sky all at once like

I had that night at the farmyard. Every so often someone would squeal, "Ooo, over there," and point to where the clouds had parted. And then we'd catch a glimpse, a patch of sky crammed with stars. A tiny bit of heaven.

"This is pretty neat," Beth said quietly.

"Yeah. Not like that other night though," I said. "The weatherman said it was supposed to be clear."

From the ground I heard someone snort.

"It doesn't matter," said Beth. Domino curled up on her stomach, I think because she wasn't wiggling as much as Lena and her stomach was bigger than mine. "I thought you didn't believe in God anymore."

Lying there staring up at the night I was thinking it was true, what I'd said that day. I could stop going to church if I wanted. I could stop praying. I could give God a different name if I wanted to.

But I couldn't just stop believing in Him. Even when I thought I didn't, He was all the time in my head. Like Grandma said, I'd believed in Him all the way already since I was just little.

"I guess I do after all," I said.

I kept waiting for the skies to clear. But instead there were more and more clouds all the time. All of a sudden the air cooled. And then fat drops of rain started plopping down all around us. Lightning flashed behind the clouds and a crack of thunder boomed right on its heels. We all jumped to our feet pretty quick, let me tell you. Only before we had time to get in the car, the clouds burst open.

It didn't just rain. It came down in buckets. Everyone was soaked through in seconds. Rain streamed through our hair and ran down our backs and dripped off our noses. In no time, rain filled the shallow ditches beside the road.

No one seemed to care. We all grinned, water pouring off us. Except Lena. She stuck out her tongue to catch the rain. Even Beth was grinning, wiping her hair back from her face.

Then Mom burst out laughing. She laughed like a little kid, surprised by something wonderful. She stepped away from the car, spread her arms wide, and laughed out loud, looking up to the sky to let the rain stream down her face. "*Mein zeit!*" she cried. "Oh my goodness gracious!"

Whooping, Jillian jumped in a puddle. Lena squealed and ran, arms out, leaping and splashing. Beth rescued Domino, tucking the shivering kitten inside her windbreaker.

What the heck, I shrugged. We all ran and splashed and spun in circles. Jillian and I grabbed each other's slippery wrists and twirled, around and around, rain glistening on our skin. Beth turned her face to the sky and opened her mouth, gulping down the rain.

Even Dad let Mom grab his hands and pull him out into the road. They swung each other around, stomping and tromping and whirling back and forth until I had to stop and watch because, Holy Moses, I never knew my Mom and Dad could dance yet.

Mom whirled toward me, collapsing with laughter. She reached out and hugged me hard.

"I didn't mean to make such a fuss over the stupid pajama party. I didn't mean to make you sad," I said, hugging her back.

"You are my sunshine, Elsie," she whispered in my ear. "You could never make me anything but happy. Don't you ever forget that."

I didn't know whether to laugh or cry. I think maybe I was doing both. Rain streamed off my face, so it was hard to tell. There was something else yet I had to know. "What did you say to Dad? You know, back at the car before?"

Mom laughed. "I said, when the heart is full, the mouth overflows." And then we laughed harder than ever.

Pretty soon the downpour fizzled away to a bit of soft, misty rain. We shook water from our hair and wiped it from our arms and legs and faces. The air was scrubbed as clean and fresh as the first day Noah stepped out of the ark.

Dear God, I prayed. *Thank you.*

27

Everything comes to an end
- except a sausage

I crept out of the house early Sunday morning.

Lena was still snoring softly yet, her mouth open, her cheeks rosy with sleep. There wasn't so much as a sound from Beth's or Dad's rooms. Everyone was making up for the sleep we'd lost the night before.

We'd all been too excited to sleep, even after Dad drove us home. We showered and changed into dry clothes while Mom and Beth made hot chocolate for everyone, with marshmallows and everything. The sun was starting to come up, before we finally crawled into our sleeping bags.

Then Mom had gone around and hugged every one of my friends. Me she saved for last.

"Thank you for the adventure," she whispered in my ear. "And you mustn't worry about me so much. I'm getting better every day. I'll be home –"

"Soon. Yeah, Mom. I know." I did know. Mom would be home again soon. Maybe this time it would be for good even.

There was a little smile in the corners of Mom's mouth. "*Nah yo*. Into your sleeping bag, *kindt*. Everything comes to an end." The smile spread to her whole mouth and she winked at me as she put out the light. "Except a sausage. It comes to two ends."

By the time we got up Saturday morning it was almost noon. Dad had taken Mom back to Eden already and smoothed things over with the doctors and nurses. He looked a little worn out from all the smoothing over, but he was helping Beth in the kitchen anyways, cooking up a whole pile of waffles with chokecherry syrup. Then Grandma came over yet, wanting to know what was happening because she'd heard a racket in the middle of the night.

"Just a little star-gazing, *Mutta*," smiled Dad.

"*Ach!* Since when do you watch stars in the rain?" she tutted.

Dad just kept smiling. "Come. Sit you *doy*, O'Lloyd." He pulled out a chair and gently pushed Grandma down into it. "You can eat breakfast with us."

"Breakfast?" she said. "Half the day already is gone!" Shaking her head, she heaved herself out of the chair, tied on an apron and went to work making her special waffle sauce. Everyone stuffed themselves with at least two waffles each – one with chokecherry syrup and one with waffle sauce. Then Dad drove us back to Eden to get our bikes, and my friends headed home.

Except Jillian and Sadie. They rode back to our place with me, to help clean out Dad's car. It was pretty gross from eleven wet people and one wet cat yet riding in it.

"I don't mind. It was worth it," said Jillian. "That was the best pajama party ever."

"At least we never got chased by the cops," grinned Sadie.

Uy uy uy. One more thing still to tell Dad about.

Probably I should've been tired out like everyone else this morning. Only I wasn't. I woke up early, even though there was no chirping anymore because when I wasn't paying attention the baby robins had grown up enough to fly away. All things come to an end, not?

For a while I lay awake thinking. I remembered what Auntie Nettie had said the day we picked berries. Maybe God could be found in lots of places. In church sure, but lots of other places, too. Like at that farmyard and in the stars and the rain and . . . all kinds of places.

I was starting to think that maybe God wasn't what I thought He was before. I mean, it wasn't like God was a person, someone you could touch and see and smell. Maybe God could even be more like a feeling inside a person.

Sometimes that feeling of God inside could be strong, like it was when we were all laughing in the rain. But sometimes a person maybe had to work hard at finding the feeling inside. Like when Mom was so sad, she probably couldn't feel God then.

My head was starting to spin again so I got out of bed. This would be a good time to practice riding with no hands.

I slipped outside, grabbed my bike and coasted down the back alley.

There wasn't much point in riding to the pool this time of day, so instead I turned left and rode all the way to First Street on the east side of town. Then I turned right and pedaled as far south as I could go, all the way to the highway that went to the States. Letting go of the handlebars, I took the corner right again, past the Sommerfeld Mennonite Church onto Valley Avenue. I could follow Valley Avenue all the way west along the edge of the town, until it came to Eden. I pedaled easily, the sun warm on my back.

The first couple of blocks were no problem. Nobody was out on the road this early. There was no one to get in my way, no corners to go around. I had to dodge a pothole in the third block and another one in the fourth block.

I edged over toward the middle of the road where there were fewer potholes. For the next three blocks I tried to stay as close to the center line as I could.

Lena, I knew, believed in God sort of like she believed in Santa Claus. He was just always there, in heaven, watching over her. He knew even before Santa Claus did whether she was naughty or nice.

Beth believed in God in a loud sort of in-your-face kind of way. Look at me, see how good I am? Though I had to give her credit. She wasn't nearly as obnoxious about it lately.

A car pulled onto the road up ahead, coming toward me. No big deal. I just leaned over to the right a little until I was back on my side of the road.

Auntie Nettie's God was a not-too-serious kind of God and Grandma Redekop believed in a no-nonsense God. Dad acted like he didn't care much for God, but really he did. Reverend Funk's God was the scariest. His God was a fire-breathing dragon one minute and a gentle father the next. You never knew who you were going to get.

Sometimes Mom's God seemed a bit like a father who never thinks anything is good enough, who always wants you to do better, like get an A instead of an A minus.

And then there was me. I didn't know what kind of God I believed in.

Up ahead was Eden already. I coasted to the corner and stopped. Fifteen blocks with no hands. I'd been too busy thinking to even make any wishes.

I couldn't really think of anything to wish for. Except for the sun to shine today, which conditions favored, because the sun was already shining. And maybe for Reverend Funk to do a good job of his sermon this morning and not talk too long, because Mom had a day pass and was coming to church with us. Then we were all going to Auntie Nettie's for dinner.

Anyways, maybe I was getting too old for wishing games. Everything comes to an end. *Nah yo.*

Or maybe not just yet. I closed my eyes and made one last wish, something big that was worth using up a fifteen-block wish for. Then I gave Mom's window a little wave and headed home. There was lots of summer left. Lots of bike rides and afternoons at the pool and pajama parties. Still one more coat of paint to put on the house. And at least one horseback ride this afternoon with Mark Giesbrecht. Who knew what all else? Anything was possible.

So I wasn't that surprised even, when I turned into the alley and coasted up to our house, to see Tommy sitting there on the back porch, waiting.

I left my bike on the lawn and sat beside him, scratching behind his torn ear. He had a few more scars than before. And he was a little thinner maybe. But otherwise he didn't look any worse for wear.

"*Voh scheent et*, Tom-cat?" I said.

He looked up at me and meowed. Loudly.

"All right already." I went inside to get him a saucer of milk, and maybe a can of tuna yet, too.

❧

Dear God,

Thanks for bringing Tommy home safe.

I'm sorry I didn't pray every day for twenty-one days, or even give up bread and meat like I said I would. See, for a while there, I didn't think I believed in you anymore. Now I know I do. I just have to figure out what that means.

I have a lot of questions. Probably I'll have a lot more yet, too. I hope you won't mind if it takes me awhile to figure things out.

In the meantime, please watch over Mom, and the rest of my family, and my friends. And Tommy, too. Please keep them safe.

That's it for now, God. Except, in case no one has told you lately, it's kind of nice to know you're around.

Amen.

Note on spellings:

Plautdietsch, or Mennonite Low German, is a wonderfully evocative language. But many of its vowel and consonant clusters would be unfamiliar to readers and therefore difficult to pronounce. For this reason, I've tried as much as possible to Anglicize the spellings phonetically, so young readers can hear the language at least close to the way it is spoken. Even so, pronunciations vary among Mennonites from different areas. People also play around with the language, combining Low German and English to make up words. And as kids growing up speaking English for the most part, we often totally ravaged the Low German language with our crude attempts at pronunciation, sometimes intentionally.

The correct spellings appear in parentheses in the glossary that follows. For these I'm indebted to Jack Thiessen's *Mennonite Low German Dictionary* as well as the second edition of Herman Rempel's *Kjenn Jie Noch Plautdietsch?* I've tried to be as accurate as possible. However, these sources are based on a different regional style than was spoken in the community in which I grew up, so I have made a few changes I felt appropriate. Any errors throughout the text or glossary are mine alone.

Glossary

ach!	Oh!
aus (auss)	as
baydel (Bädel)	scoundrel
bayn (Been)	legs
beksen (Betjsen)	pants
best (best)	are
blous gout (blooss goot)	just good, only good
bubbat (Bobbat)	cake-like raisin dressing for chicken
dan	then
daugnichts (Daugnijchts)	good-for-nothing
daut (daut)	that, it, the
dayt (deit)	does
deevilschinda (Diewelschinda)	devil. Schinda is a skinner, and the word is often used as a mild form of devil. The combination of two words referring to the devil is a vulgar reference.
deh (dee)	that; also he, she, him, her, they, them
doa, doy (doa)	there; doy is a family variation, part of longstanding joke

dummkopp (Dommkopp)	blockhead, fool
du (dü)	you
em (emm)	in
en (een)	a, an, one
es	is
faspa (Vaspa)	afternoon coffee or light lunch, a Mennonite institution
ferekt (veretjt)	crazy
fuy (fuj)	phooey
gaunz	totally, completely
glommskopp (Glommskopp)	blockhead, idiot; literally, "cottage cheese head"
goondach (Goondach)	good day
gurknaze (Gurtjenäs)	big nose; literally, "cucumber nose"
hollopchee (Holloptsee)	cabbage rolls
Hallemoss! (Hallemos!)	Holy Moses!
hundt (Hund)	dog
kella (Tjalla)	cellar
kielke (Tjieltje)	homemade noodles
kint (Tjind)	child
klive (kleiwe)	to scratch or claw
knackzote (Knacksot)	sunflower seeds
kringel (Tjrinjel)	pretzel-shaped, twisted buns
knippsbrat (Tjnippsbrat)	crokinole

knippse (tjnippse)	to flick the finger from the thumb
knirps (Tjnirps)	twirp, cocky little fellow
kohta (Kohta)	tom cat
kressberren (Tjressbäaren)	gooseberries
lite (leet)	sorry
louse (looss)	loose, untied. "Waut es looss?" is a common phrase meaning "What is wrong?" Literally, "What is loose?"
me (mie)	me, myself
meyahl (Mejahl)	girl
mouse (Mooss)	cold, stewed fruit soup
mumke (Mumtje)	woman
mutta (Mutta)	mother
mein zeit!	a High German expression meaning, "Oh my!" or "My gosh!"
nay (nä)	no
nah yo (na jo)	literally, well yes, but its meaning depends on how it's used
nich (nijch)	not
nusht (nuscht)	nothing
och vaut (Och waut!)	Tut-tut! Exclamation of impatience or mild denial

ootyeklivft (ütjekleiwft)	run away, beat it; literally "has scratched out"
ootyepoopt (ütjepüpt)	tired out, pooped
piroshki (Perieschtje)	baked turnover-like pie with meat or fruit in it
platz (Plautz)	Large, flat cake topped with fruit
Plautdietsch	Low German; literally "flat German"
plumen mouse (Plümemoos)	Cold plum and dried fruit soup, a regular Mennonite Sunday dish
pudel (Puddel)	puddle
putzendonna (Putzendoona)	mischief-maker, joker
rollkuchen (Rollkuaken)	deep-fried dough strips or fritters, commonly served with watermelon; literally, "roll cookies"
schauntboa (schaundboa)	shameful
scheent (schient)	shines
schentlich (schendlijch)	disgraceful, scandalous
schlap (schlape)	to drag
schindashin hite (schindashen heet)	devilish hot
schmack gout (schmatje goot)	tastes good

schmauntfat (Schmaundfat)	cream gravy
schmocke bayn (schmock Been)	nice legs
schmungestrasse (Schmunjestrasse)	lover's lane
schnetke conference (Schnettje-Konferenz)	a gathering of gossips, literally a "biscuit conference"
schnigglefritz (Schnidjelfrits)	teasing reference, usually to a young boy
schozzle (Schosel)	dolt, dunderhead, someone who acts silly
schnoddanaze (Schnoddanäs)	young know-it-all; literally, "snot-nose"
schvack (schwack)	weak
summaborscht (Sommaborscht)	sorrel and potato soup. Literally "summer soup"
Taunte (Taunte)	aunt
tubbdook (Tobbdüak)	dishrag
Uy uy uy (Uj uj uj)	exclamation; My, my, my!
varenika (Wrennetje)	perogies; dough packets usually filled with cottage cheese
vaut (waut)	what
vea (wäa)	who
vea es doa (waä es doa?)	who is there?
vite dee (weehte die)	mind your own business; literally, "know yourself"

vooa (woa)	where
voh (woo)	how
vota (Wota)	water

| yung (Jung) | boy |

Selected phrases:

Daut deit mie leet.	I am sorry
Dee hucke sitj oppe Uahren.	She sit herself on her ears.
Schwack auss een Tobbdüak.	Weak as a dishcloth.
voh scheent et? (Woo schient et?)	How are things? Literally, "How shines it?" A common Mennonite greeting.
Wota emm Tjalla Betjsen.	Water in cellar pants, meaning pants that are too short.

Acknowledgments

For the Low German sayings and "upgemixed" English, I have my memories of growing up in a Mennonite community to thank, but even more so I thank the many family and friends who helped jog my memories and added their own to the mix. My mother, especially, suffered through many interruptions to patiently answer one question after another. She went so far as to try and teach me correct Plautdietsch pronunciations, until finally throwing up her hands in disgust and declaring, "That's the best your tongue will do." My heartfelt thanks go out to her and my siblings – Iris, Bill, Kathy, and Becky – and to Barb and Aron, Nancy, Susan, Jocelyn, Jeannette, Linda, and Connie. For some thirty years now, these childhood friends have continued to welcome me back on intermittent visits to my hometown. They have shown me a grace that never fails to enrich my appreciation for my roots.

As well as these personal sources, I'm also indebted to several texts, including Jack Thiessen's *Mennonite Low German Dictionary*, Herman Rempel's *Kjenn Jie Noch Plautdietsch?*, *The Windmill Turning*, by Victor Carl Friesen, and Armin Wiebe's *The Salvation of Yasch Siemens*, which has left me laughing myself half dead so many times over the years.

Special thanks go to Kathryn Cole and Kathy Lowinger for their editorial insight, enthusiasm, and patience. I feel fortunate to have had the benefit of Kathryn Cole's deft editorial hand in making Elsie's story all it could be.